"We're going to be married!" she insisted

Lara's face became shadowed with hurt as she felt Jordan's anger.

"And that means I automatically stop being aware of other women's beauty? Grow up, Lara," he bit out coldly. "I'm as aware of Cathy's desirability now as I have always been."

"You still...want her?" Lara was very pale.

"Yes!"

For a moment she was stunned with shock. "I thought...but, Jordan, we're going to be *married*...."

"All that proves is that I desire you more than I desire Cathy."

"Desire," she echoed in distress. "Is that all you feel for me?"

His mouth tightened ominously. "Lara, don't turn into a clinging vine. I warn you, I won't be tied down!"

Books by Carole Mortimer

HARLEQUIN PRESENTS

These books may be available at your local bookseller.

For a list of all titles currently available,
send your name and address to:

Harlequin Reader Service
P.O. Box 52040, Phoenix, AZ 85072-2040
Canadian address: P.O. Box 2800, Postal Station A,
5170 Yonge St., Willowdale, Ont. M2N 5T5

CAROLE MORTIMER

hard to get

Harlequin Books

TORONTO • NEW YORK • LONDON
AMSTERDAM • PARIS • SYDNEY • HAMBURG
STOCKHOLM • ATHENS • TOKYO • MILAN

For
John and Matthew

Harlequin Presents first edition September 1984
ISBN 0-373-10724-2

Original hardcover edition published in 1984
by Mills & Boon Limited

CHAPTER ONE

'WHO is that man, Daddy?'

'What man, Lara?' he sounded preoccupied, still disgruntled over the fact that she had just beaten him at his favourite sport.

They were seated in the club-house of her father's exclusive golf-club in the south of England, her father drowning his sorrows in his whisky glass, her own white wine being in the form of a celebration drink. She and her father often played golf together, but this had been the first time she had ever managed to beat him. That knowledge filled her with glee.

'The one over there with Gary Ridgeway.' She made a point of not looking in the direction of the two men as they stood talking together at the bar.

Her father wasn't so tactful and, turned to look straight at the two men. 'Good-looking chap,' he murmured softly. 'Vaguely familiar,' he added in a puzzled voice. 'But no, I don't think I recognise him.'

'Oh,' she frowned her disappointment.

'Lara!' he gave her a warning look. 'Haven't you learnt your lesson? The scandal of Rex Maynard is only just dying down.'

She blushed painfully red, painful because she knew her father was right to be concerned after the episode of Rex. She had made a fool of herself over him, little knowing that all the time he was seeing her he was also assessing her jewellery and plotting with a maid in the house to steal the most worthwhile pieces. It had been like something out of a Victorian drama, but it had really happened!

Rex had seemed so nice when she met him at a party in town, had been an amusing and attentive companion. And she had been made to look such an idiot when he and her maid had been caught in the act of stealing her jewellery. It had been a lesson she would never forget, especially as the maid had turned out to be Rex's wife! The newspapers had had fun with her for weeks, and the gossip columns still referred to her relationship with 'her maid's husband'.

'This man hardly looks like a thief, Daddy,' she drawled.

The man who had her full attention looked far from in need of money, his clothes casual but expensively cut and tailored, the narrow-fitting trousers a very pale blue, the navy blue sweater obviously cashmere, a perfect foil for the overlong silver-blond hair, although it didn't seem to be an affectation the man nurtured, conceit seeming to be the least of his vices. That particular shade of hair, neither blond nor silver but somewhere attractively in between, was a strange colour for a man, and if it had been on a woman Lara would have said it was dyed. As it was, it suited this man perfectly; his skin was a deep healthy bronze in contrast, his eyes the deepest blue she had ever seen, almost navy from this distance. His nose jutted out arrogantly, his mouth strong and firm, his jaw thrust out at a confident angle. And he was tall, over six feet she would have said, leanly built, but muscularly so, no superfluous flesh on his body despite the mid-thirties she guessed him to be.

She had seen him as soon as she and her father entered the club fifteen minutes ago, her own grey jumper and black fitted trousers complementing her slender figure perfectly, her long straight black hair reaching down past her shoulders, gleaming with a deep ebony sheen, the fringe feathered back from a centre parting. Her make-up was subtly light, a dark blue eye-shadow on her lids, her lashes naturally long and silky, her eyes a light grey, looking strangely luminous with the unusual black ring around the iris, her cheekbones highlighted with a dark blusher, her nose short and straight, a dark plum lip-gloss shaping her mouth.

She knew without conceit that she was attractive, and yet when she had greeted Gary Ridgeway at the bar as she and her father entered the club-house the man with him had virtually ignored her. Oh, the navy blue eyes had moved over her dispassionately for several seconds, and then she was calmly dismissed as he turned away.

And Lara wasn't used to being dismissed! She had been able to attract any man she wanted since she had been fifteen years old, and in the last five years no man had ignored her the way this one dared to.

'I think I'll just go and have a word with Gary,' she told her father in a preoccupied voice.

'Lara!'

She looked down at her father as she stood up. 'Mm?' she asked vaguely.

'You can't just go over there and interrupt them,' he frowned darkly.

'Of course I can.' She gave him a confident smile before strolling across the room, knowing she was the centre of male attention as she did so. Except for the man with the navy blue eyes. But Gary Ridgeway had been asking her out for the last month or so, so a little encouragement while she got to know the other man wouldn't do any harm. 'Hello, Gary,' she greeted silkily as she joined the two men. 'I'm not interrupting anything, am I?' She gave a smile that said she was sure she wasn't, and even if she were she was sure she would be forgiven for it.

'Our conversation was private,' the man with the silver-blond hair told her abruptly.

Lara's confidence wavered for only a moment before she gave a dazzling smile. 'I won't keep you long,' she told him huskily, finding he was taller than she had first thought, her own five feet eight inch frame only reaching to that strong jaw even in her three-inch-heeled sandals.

He nodded distantly and turned back to Gary. 'I'll be back in a few minutes, there's someone I need to talk to. Excuse me,' he bit out in Lara's general direction before striding off.

'Oh, but—' she sighed her disappointment as he didn't even falter, joining two couples a short distance away, smiling charmingly at the older of the two women, the still-attractive blonde blossoming under this exclusive attention. 'Your friend isn't very—sociable,' she drawled waspishly to the man at her side. Gary was the epitome of everything that was tall, dark and handsome—and he knew it. It could be a little embarrassing to have a date who was prettier than you! And she wished now that the man with the navy blue eyes had gone so that she too could leave, having no wish to turn down yet another of Gary's invitations.

'Jordan?' He looked at the other man consideringly. 'I find him a very sociable chap.' He looked back at her with mocking eyes. 'But I'm glad that on this occasion he didn't feel that way.'

She gave a mental groan. Gary certainly didn't have an original line in seduction, and she had heard it too often the last month to be in the least impressed. How to get away, that was the problem. 'Jordan?' she prompted frantically.

'Jordan Sinclair,' he provided uninterestedly. 'He's in property.'

'Really?' Her own interest in the man was still as deep. 'I haven't seen him at the club before.'

'He's my guest, not a member, although he hopes to be soon. I shall be proposing him.'

'Really?' she said again. 'Does he live around here or in London?'

'Did you come over here solely to talk about Jordan?' Gary snapped. 'And I thought it was my charm that attracted you,' he sneered angrily.

Lara could have told him he didn't have any, that he had a good physique and looks to recommend him and very little else. But this man was a business acquaintance of her father, and despite her father's thoughts to the contrary, she knew this man only too well. It had been through her father that the two of them had met, and although Gary was forty to her twenty he never lost an opportunity to make known his attraction to her, and always far away from her father's notice. He was a man to be wary of.

'I was only curious about Mr Sinclair,' she dismissed lightly. 'Did you win your game?' she changed the subject, knowing this man enjoyed nothing more than talking about himself.

'Jordan did,' he admitted with reluctance.

'Are you sure you want him to become a member?' she teased, unable to resist the taunt.

Gary didn't respond to her humour; he was one of those people who saw little to laugh about in themselves. 'I had a bad day,' he dismissed. 'How about joining me for dinner tonight, Lara?'

It was the invitation she had been hoping to avoid, but his relationship with her father meant she couldn't be rude to him. 'Not tonight, I'm afraid,' she refused.

'Daddy is giving a dinner party, and he expects me to be there as his hostess. Some other time, Gary,' she added hastily as he frowned. 'I have to go now, I can see Daddy is getting restless,' She could see Gary was far from pleased with this evasion of his invitation, but she managed to make her escape before the situation could become too awkward.

'Well?' her father mocked as she rejoined him at their table, sipping languidly at her white wine.

'His name is Jordan Sinclair and he's in the property business,' she told him lightly.

'You didn't get that from the man himself,' he derided. 'Not too impressed with you, was he, Lara?' he mocked indulgently.

She watched as Jordan Sinclair rejoined Gary, and the two of them left a few seconds later, without the navy blue eyes having looked at her once since he had excused himself so abruptly and left her alone with Gary. 'Not yet.' She turned back to her father after watching the impressive figure of Jordan Sinclair fold itself behind the wheel of a red Ferrari, driving the fast car out of the club car park with a style that spoke of a confident driver. Well, she was far from lacking in confidence herself, and Jordan Sinclair intrigued her very much. 'But he will be,' she smiled knowingly.

'Lara!'

'Yes, Daddy?' she enquired with sweet innocence.

He sighed at the determination in her luminous grey eyes. 'Don't get involved in something you can't handle,' he pleaded, a man who blamed the abundance of grey in his own black hair on the fact that he had been in a perpetual state of worry since Lara became a teenager and decided the opposite sex was a lot more interesting than any of the expensive toys she owned. He was still a handsome man at fifty-five, and when he made com-

plaints about her impulsive behaviour ageing him she
merely told him how distinguished he looked with the
grey wings of hair at his temples. 'And Jordan Sinclair
doesn't look like a man any woman could control.'

The determination turned to challenge. 'No?'

'I think we should be going.' Her father swallowed the
last of his whisky, knowing from experience that the
more one argued with Lara the more determined she
became. 'We have guests this evening, remember?'

'Yes,' she replied in a preoccupied voice, her thoughts
racing. A dinner party, what more natural way to get to
know someone?

'Lara?' her father prompted, already standing up,
tall and thin, with a boundless energy that had made
him the head of the hotel empire he now owned and
ran.

'Sorry,' she stood up gracefully, 'I was just thinking.'

'That's what I'm afraid of,' he grimaced. 'Leave this
one alone, hmm?'

Lara raised dark brows. 'You make me sound like a
man-eater!'

'If by that you mean no man is safe from you, then yes,
that's exactly what you are. Lara,' he sighed, 'the man
looked out of your league.'

'Don't be silly, Daddy, men aren't in leagues, they're
just available or unavailable. And Gary didn't say anything about Jordan Sinclair being unavailable,' she
smiled her satisfaction.

Her father shook his head in exasperation, giving up
any hope of distracting her from her interest in Jordan
Sinclair, concentrating on manoeuvring his Jaguar sa-
loon on to the motorway. But he made a mental note to
check out the silver-haired man who had so attracted his
daughter. Lara might think she lived a very free and
independent life, but since Rex Maynard had so upset

her life he had had a close watch kept on the friends she made, wanting no repeat of her humiliation.

It was as well he couldn't see his daughter half an hour later. The two of them were back at the London town house they shared alone now, Lara's stepmother having died five years ago. The new telephone directory was open in front of her as she searched through the J. Sinclairs for the most likely address of the man she had met at the golf-club. In the end she tried all the numbers listed under that initial and name, receiving irate responses to her cheerful greeting, and not one of them the husky voice of the man with the navy blue eyes.

After forty minutes' frantic telephoning she had to admit defeat. Jordan Sinclair really must be new in town; he wasn't even in the telephone book. And she didn't have any more time to waste, the dinner party was supposed to start in an hour's time, and she had to be at her father's side once the guests began to arrive, having acted as his hostess for the last two years since she had left school.

All of the guests were known to her, and she was laughing at something Paul Davis had said when her gaze clashed and held with that of a late arrival. Jordan Sinclair! And he was with Cathy Thomas, a wealthy divorcee. And from the way she was caressing his arm as they talked with her father Lara had a feeling their relationship was intimate. Damn! Cathy was the original gay divorcee, but her men usually lasted for months.

Lara excused herself from Paul's side, moving determinedly to be with her father, secure in the knowledge that the royal blue dress she wore clung revealingly to her naked breasts and narrow hips, the light wool of the gown swinging gently against her body as she moved. Her make-up was slightly heavier tonight, although she still looked fresh and beautiful, her lips glistening provocatively with a dark lip-gloss, her perfume subtly seductive.

'Cathy! How lovely to see you again,' she greeted the other woman softly. Cathy was her senior by fifteen years, a small voluptuous redhead who made no secret of the fact that she lived very well on the maintenance her ex-husband paid her, and that she had no intention of losing that by marrying again. But that didn't stop her having numerous affairs. And Jordan Sinclair was obviously the latest man in her life. *Damn!*

'You too, Lara,' Cathy said more coolly, the two of them having little, if nothing, in common. At least, they hadn't, until Jordan came along! 'I don't believe you know Jordan.' She still held on to his arm with an obvious show of possession.

Grey eyes met navy blue ones, only cool enquiry in the latter, although Lara wasn't so sure her own gaze was as cool. The black evening suit made Jordan's hair look more silver than blond, his skin a deep bronze against the snowy white shirt. He looked magnificent, towering over her father as he stood next to him, and Lara's pulse-rate gave an unexpected leap.

'You're wrong,' she gave Cathy a saccharine smile. 'Jordan and I met this afternoon—didn't we?' she looked at him beneath sooty lashes, knowing how fascinating her eyes looked from that angle, the black circle around the grey more noticeable as she looked up. She had practised the pose endlessly in the mirror when she was fifteen, and over the years she had come to know the effect it had on men, had driven the cook's son wild with it when she was sixteen, before she moved on to more interesting quary. 'At the golf-club,' she reminded him as neither her words nor her provocative glance had any effect on the cool expression.

The navy blue eyes flickered over her uninterestedly,

the dark blond brows raising questioningly. 'Did we?' he drawled.

Lara was disconcerted, and too surprised to hide it. 'With Gary,' she frowned. 'In the club-house.'

He seemed to give the matter serious thought, and then finally he nodded. 'I do seem to remember a young girl coming over to talk to him now . . . But I would hardly say we met,' he mocked. 'I believe I left to speak to an acquaintance while you were with Gary.'

'Gary Ridgeway?' Cathy taunted Lara. 'I would hardly have said he was your type, darling.'

Lara managed to maintain her composure at the taunt, although mentally she admitted it had taken a serious knock the last few minutes. 'Young girl' was hardly the way she thought of herself, and to be called that by a man she found so attractive did nothing for her ego. 'He was yours a few months ago,' she heard the bitchy comment leave her lips with a feeling of dismay. No matter how much Cathy's relationship with Jordan annoyed her she shouldn't have insulted one of her father's guests in her home. And she knew by the stern glint in her father's eyes that she would hear more on the subject later.

'Maybe so,' Cathy patted her already perfectly styled red hair. 'But isn't he a little old for you, dear? Or do I mean you're too young for him?' She gave a light dismissive laugh that said it wasn't really important anyway—she was confident she had nothing to fear from the young girl. 'How did the game go, darling?' She turned to Jordan.

'Fair,' came the curt reply, although the eyes had warmed to dark navy as he smiled at the other woman.

'But Gary said you won.' Lara didn't like being excluded from the conversation.

Jordan met her gaze coolly. 'I did.'

'But—'

'Gary had an off day,' he shrugged.

'Maybe I could challenge you to a round some day?' she pursued. 'Gary says you're going to become a member.'

'Maybe, Miss . . .?' he raised dark blond brows questioningly.

'Schofield, Lara Schofield.' Her tone was impatient that he didn't already know who she was.

'My daughter,' her father put in lightly. 'And don't take up the challenge for golf, Mr Sinclair,' he warned dryly. 'Lara has a good handicap.'

'I have one of five myself,' the younger man drawled.

'Really?' Her father's interest deepened. 'Then perhaps we could play a round together some time?'

Jordan nodded. 'I'd like that.'

'Good, good,' her father beamed.

Lara fumed as Cathy and Jordan strolled off to join several other people across the room. He would 'like' to play a round of golf with her father, with her it was only 'maybe'! Having to chase a man wasn't something she enjoyed or wanted, never having had to do it before. And Jordan Sinclair certainly wasn't making it easy for her either! He was laughing huskily now at something Cathy had said, the coldness with which he usually spoke to *her* completely gone. Could it be that he really didn't like her?

'Not so easy, is it, Lara?' her father mused, looking at the other man with admiring eyes. 'Cathy isn't going to let him go in a hurry,' he murmured as the other woman glowed up at her companion. 'Not that he looks as if he wants to go anywhere,' he chuckled as Jordan's head bent and he briefly claimed provocatively pouting red lips.

'She's too old for him,' Lara snapped waspishly,

having revised her first impression of Jordan being in his mid-thirties; he looked no more than thirty.

'That doesn't seem to bother him,' her father smiled down at her. 'A bit of a surprise him turning up here tonight,' he added thoughtfully.

'Yes.' Her mouth was tight as she continued to watch the intimacy between Cathy and Jordan.

Her father chuckled softly as he followed her gaze. 'And I always thought your eyes were grey!'

She turned to him with a puzzled frown. 'They are— Daddy!' she sighed her impatience as she saw the humour glinting in his eyes. 'It isn't funny.'

'I didn't think so this afternoon when you showed such an interest in a handsome stranger, but I don't think I need fear Jordan Sinclair. You obviously aren't his type, button,' he lightly tapped her slightly upturned nose.

'Men don't have a "type",' she snapped. 'Women either, for that matter. And I haven't given up on Mr Sinclair.' Not by a long way, she vowed mentally.

Her father shrugged. 'As I said, I don't think you're in any danger from Jordan Sinclair. And if you intend chasing the man,' he added sternly, 'make sure you do it without sniping at one of our guests.'

She flushed at the rebuke. 'I'm sorry about that, Daddy. But they both seemed so—so patronising!'

'The man is too old for you, darling,' her father sympathised. 'In manner if not in years. Why don't you go and talk to poor Nigel? He's been watching you with hungry eyes ever since he arrived.'

Nigel Wentworth. Two years her senior at twenty-two, tall and fair, good-looking in an eager sort of way, heir to his father's chain of men's clothing stores. Her father approved of him because he was as rich as she was, would one day take over from his father. Lara knew he had been in love with her for the last few months, that he would probably ask her to marry him one day. As far as she was concerned he came in useful when she needed a partner to go to a party or the theatre, but other than that she preferred to avoid him. The eager love he showed was stifling, and the thought of spending the rest of her life with him was unacceptable to her.

Nevertheless, he could come in useful this evening, a salve to her wounded ego. 'Okay,' she agreed lightly, much to her father's surprise.

His eyes narrowed at this unexpected willingness to entertain a man Lara had always maintained was a 'stupid boy'. 'Lara?' he questioned warily.

Wide grey eyes looked back at him guilelessly. 'Yes, Daddy?'

He gave a weary groan, shaking his head. 'I wish Marion were here now, she always knew how to make you see sense.'

For a few silent moments they shared their loss of Marion Schofield, Lara's stepmother, Joseph's dearly-loved second wife for many years.

Lara's own mother had died in childbirth, and two years later her father had married Marion Saunders, a childless widow of thirty. It had been an idyllic marriage, and at only two Lara had readily accepted the tall golden-haired woman as her mother, and the two of them were very close until Marion had been tragically killed in a riding accident shortly after Lara's fifteenth birthday.

Straight after this their country estate had been closed up, and Lara and her father had moved into the London house. The estate was always kept ready for their use even now, but Lara could count the times on one hand that they had been there the last five years. Neither of them could bear to be for long in the place where the three of them had been so happy for thirteen years, and the stables were empty now, a bleak reminder that her father had ordered all the horses to be sold after his wife was killed. In his rage and agony he had ordered the horse Marion had been riding to be destroyed, and it was only when Lara, equally shocked and heartbroken, had persuaded him that it hadn't been the horse's fault, that Marion wouldn't have wanted the magnificent chestnut stallion destroyed, that he had relented and instead ordered that to be sold too.

Five years hadn't dulled her father's love for his wife; Marion had been a beautiful woman, both on the inside as well as the outside. No woman could ever take her place in his affection or his arms, and so the hotels he already owned all over the world had become his life's interest, the existence of Lara the only thing that had kept him sane since Marion died.

'I still miss her too, Daddy.' Lara grasped his hand now.

'Yes,' he acknowledged gruffly, seeming to come out of the daze as he realised their surroundings. 'We'd better circulate, darling. As hosts we're decidedly lacking in manners.'

She nodded. 'I'll go and talk to Nigel.'

Her father touched her arm lightly. 'And stay away from Cathy and Jordan, hmm?'

Her eyes widened with innocent reproach. 'I couldn't do that, Daddy. They are our guests, you know.'

He sighed at her determination. 'Well, try and behave yourself at least.'

'Of course!' Her tone sharpened with indignation. 'Don't I always?' The look her father gave her before she walked off spoke volumes!

Her poor father—he had never quite known what to do with her once left alone with her as a teenager, and now he had no chance of controlling her. Asking her to stay away from Jordan Sinclair was like asking bees to stay away from the flowers! He intrigued her more than any other man she knew, and she wouldn't let him treat her like some irritating schoolgirl.

As usual Nigel was eager for her company, talking at a fast rate in an effort to try and hold her attention, terrified she was going to become bored with him and walk off. She could have put his mind at rest about that, he *always* bored her. She was aware only of his voice droning on in the background, murmuring words of encouragement in acknowledgement in all the right places, her whole attention on Cathy Thomas and her attractive companion.

She became more convinced than ever that the couple were lovers, their every gesture and movement indicated as much. Up until now Lara had liked her men easily manageable, and the hint of a physical relationship without actually making any promises was a sure way to keep a man interested and attentive. That didn't look as if it would work with Jordan Sinclair, the sensuality about his firm mouth seeming to indicate the need for a physical relationship with his women. And just because she had never been that deeply involved with a man it didn't mean she wasn't willing to be; she wanted Jordan Sinclair any way she could get him.

'What do you think of the idea, Lara?'

'Mm?' she turned vaguely back to Nigel, aware by the intensity of his expression that she had missed something of importance. 'Sorry?' she prompted brightly.

'My parents would like to meet you,' he obviously repeated, the expression in his brown eyes hopeful. 'Does the idea appeal to you?'

Like being shot at dawn! Lara had heard of Carolyn and Seymour Wentworth, of the way Carolyn was completely subservient to her tycoon husband, and the idea of being vetted by them as a prospective wife for Nigel didn't appeal to her at all. She might have been friendly with Nigel, might even have been out with him occasionally, but she had never given him the impression that she intended marrying him.

'It doesn't,' she told him bluntly.

'But—'

'Really, Nigel, don't be so intense,' she dismissed lightly. 'Meeting parents is so old-fashioned,' she added, to soften the blow. 'We don't need that sort of thing, do we?'

'Well . . .'

She put her arm through the crook of his. 'Baines is just going to announce dinner,' she smiled.

'But—'

'Come along, Nigel,' she dragged him across the room. 'I'm hungry!' She was also desperate to drop the subject of meeting his parents. She would have to avoid him for a couple of weeks or so, and with luck he would have stopped being so serious by then; she wouldn't want to stop seeing him completely. Why on earth had he had to become so intense? she thought miserably.

Her frowning grey eyes were raised to meet contemptuous navy blue ones, and for a moment she was sure her expression became blank, taken aback at finding Jordan Sinclair watching her when she had thought him unaware of her existence. Then she smiled, a slow seductive smile designed to entice—only to have him turn his back on her.

Damn the man, what had she done to make him dislike her in this way? It wasn't the usual reaction men had to her, in fact she could never remember having such a negative one before, being always confident of her own attraction.

She might as well not have existed for all the notice

Jordan Sinclair took of her during dinner, the two women, Cathy on one side, Pamela Grierson, another single woman, on the other, claiming all of his attention. Not that he seemed to mind, laughing softly several times, obviously enjoying both the meal and the company. He was a man most women would find attractive, a challenge, and Cathy visibly preened in front of Pamela because she was the one who held his physical interest.

Although that wasn't necessarily a permanent thing; Jordan seemed to enjoy Pamela's interest in him too. He would be a man who liked women, and from what Lara could judge through dinner, he wasn't averse to having more than one in his life at the same time.

When Pamela disappeared to the bathroom after dinner to freshen her make-up, and Cathy followed a few minutes later, a determined glint in her sparkling blue eyes, Lara had a feeling the two women would be discussing more than the weather.

But she wasn't concerned with Cathy or Pamela at the moment, only by the fact that their temporary absence had left Jordan alone, if only briefly; there appeared to be several other women here who would eagerly take their place. Lara was determined it was going to be her.

'Excuse me, Nigel,' she turned to give him a vague smile, having been unsuccessful in shaking him off after dinner, making her more determined to avoid him for a few weeks. 'There's someone I have to talk to.'

'But—'

'Circulate, Nigel,' she encouraged sharply at his almost hurt expression. 'That's what parties are for.'

He grasped her hand. 'But I only came here to see you.'

She patted his hand consolingly. 'And you've seen me. But I have other guests, I can't let you monopolise me all evening.'

'Lara—'

'Go and talk to my father, Nigel,' she encouraged mischievously, knowing that no matter how much her father approved of Nigel as a companion for her, he bored him out of his mind too, always insisting on how good his prospects were, and how he was destined to take over from his father in a couple of years' time.

Nigel brightened at her suggestion. 'I'll see you later, then,' he said hopefully.

'Probably,' Lara replied noncommittally, anxious to get to Jordan Sinclair's side before Cathy or Pamela returned, both women still vying for his attention.

He stood alone near the grand piano in the lounge, although he didn't look as if it particularly bothered him, a smile of amusement on his lips, as he slowly sipped the brandy in his bulbous glass.

'Hello.' Lara looked at him beneath lowered lashes as dark blue eyes were turned on her, feeling a thrill of excitement just being near him like this.

He nodded abruptly, the blue gaze swinging across the room to where her father and Nigel were engaged in conversation. 'Your boy-friend?' he drawled.

'Heavens, no!' she dismissed callously. 'Just a friend. Do you play?' she asked interestedly.

'Sorry?' he arched dark blond brows at her, his humour having faded as soon as she joined him.

She frowned her irritation with this fact. 'You were looking at the piano, I wondered if you played?'

'No,' came the abrupt answer.

Lara searched about in her mind for something else to talk about; Jordan Sinclair didn't exactly encourage her into conversation!

'You?' he bit out.

'No,' she laughed her relief that he was actually

making some effort to talk to her. 'It belonged to my stepmother, she played very well.'

'Played?' he prompted hardly.

Lara nodded. 'She's dead now. Daddy can't bring himself to part with the piano, even though there's no one to play it now.'

'I had no idea your father was a widower.'

'Twice now,' she nodded. 'Although he misses Marion the most. So do I; she was a wonderful mother to me. She brought me up as if I were her own from the time I was two years old, when she and Daddy were married. I—er—I'm glad you came here tonight,' she gave him that smouldering look beneath lowered lashes once again, her chagrin intensified as he still seemed immune to her. It wasn't normal, damn him!

'Really?' he drawled.

'Yes,' she rushed on, determined this man should be aware of her interest in him. 'After I met you at the club earlier—after I saw you,' she amended at his taunting look, 'I tried to telephone you.'

His eyes narrowed to questioning slits. 'Indeed? And why should you want to do that?'

Lara shrugged, aware that the movement brought attention to the provocative thrust of her pert young breasts. 'I thought you might like to come to a dinner party.'

'As you can see,' he gave an arrogant inclination of his head, 'I do like to attend dinner parties.'

'With Cathy.'

His mouth twisted. 'Yes.'

She sighed. 'I had intended for you to have a different—companion,' she murmured throatily, 'but I couldn't find your number in the book.'

'Cathy wouldn't have liked that, Miss Schofield—and neither would I.' His voice hardened from the silky purr to icy contempt. 'I like to choose my own women, which is also one of the reasons my telephone number is ex-directory. That way it's known only to the people I choose to give it to. Do I make myself clear, Miss Schofield?'

No one had ever called her 'Miss Schofield' in quite that way before, with a mixture of contempt and dislike, the strange blue eyes looking at her coldly. Lara moistened her lips nervously. 'Does that mean you wouldn't tell it to me?'

'Not even if you asked,' he bit out.

Her eyes flashed. 'I wasn't about to!'

'No?' he taunted.

'No!' pride came to her rescue. 'I don't need to chase after a man, Mr Sinclair. Nigel may only be a friend, but there are plenty of other men who aren't, and won't be.' Her chin rose haughtily. 'If you'll excuse me . . .'

'Without hesitation,' he scorned.

Lara turned and walked away, hoping that no one looking at her bright smile would see the tears she was blinking back.

CHAPTER TWO

'HAVE you seen anything more of Jordan Sinclair?' her father asked casually after dinner at their home one evening three weeks later.

Had she seen anything of him? She seemed to do nothing else! Everywhere she went, to the theatre, parties, Jordan Sinclair was there, and always with Cathy Thomas, the other woman more possessive of him than ever. Trying to avoid Jordan Sinclair these last few weeks had been like trying to avoid her father—and she saw him every day of her life!

And she wanted to avoid Jordan Sinclair, more than she had ever wanted to avoid any one else in her life. She had never been as insulted as she had been by him, and although he was the most fascinating man she had met in a long time she didn't need his sort of insults. Her ego had taken a severe beating the night of her father's dinner party, and it had taken three weeks of attentive male companions—not Nigel, she had kept to her decision not to see him for a few weeks!—to restore her faith in her own attraction.

'Have you?' She raised dark brows, looking fresh and attractive in a cream lace evening dress that emphasised the thick darkness of her long black hair, caught back at her slender nape to give her a look of delicate fragility.

Her father shrugged, enjoying a cigar with his brandy. 'I played golf with him today, actually.'

Lara instantly tensed. 'Yes?'

'He won,' her father grimaced.

That didn't altogether surprise her; Jordan Sinclair

would be a man who liked to win at everything he did.
'Maybe he gets more practice at it than you,' she consoled.

'I don't think so,' he sighed. 'By all accounts he's a man who works a damned sight harder than he plays.'

As she had had opportunity to see how hard he played the last few weeks she knew he must work very hard indeed. 'Where did he come from?' she frowned. 'I'd never seen him before a month ago.'

'Apparently his was basically a northern based company, it was only recently, last month in fact, that he moved down to London.'

'In that case Cathy moved fast,' she said dryly.

'Or Jordan did,' her father taunted just as dryly.

Lara blushed. 'Yes.'

'You didn't answer my question.' Her father was watching her with narrowed eyes. 'Have you seen anything of him?'

'Only casually, at parties,' she dismissed lightly. 'And always with Cathy. Why?' she frowned at his interest.

'I was just curious—'

'You aren't still fussing about Rex Maynard, are you?' she snapped irritably. 'Really, Daddy, I can't keep apologising for that one mistake! I only—'

'Peace!' he held up his hands in smiling submission. 'I just felt I should tell you a little about our Mr Sinclair,' he sobered. 'He's a hard man. He was adopted by the Sinclairs when he was fourteen; God knows where and with whom he spent the early days of his life. In any event, he wasn't grateful for his adoption, and he ran away on more than one occasion. When he was eighteen he succeeded, and never went back. Whatever he's been doing the last twelve years it gave him the capital and drive to carve himself a property empire.' Her father's expression was grim. 'He's the sort of man who'll trample other people into the dust to achieve his objective. And I would rather you stayed away from him. You may think Rex was a bastard, but believe me, he was a weak little kitten compared to some of the things I've heard about Jordan Sinclair!'

Lara knew all about Jordan's cruelty, had witnessed it first-hand, and yet knowing of his background, of the hardships he must have suffered during his childhood, somehow made her understand him more. He had been rude and hurtful to her at the dinner party *after* she had told him about her happy childhood. With his background that was enough to make anyone bitter.

'Lara?' her father frowned at her preoccupied expression.

'Sorry,' she gave him a bright meaningless smile. 'What you've told me is very interesting, Daddy,' she dismissed in light tones. 'Although I can't imagine where you get your information from . . .' she eyed him mockingly.

He had the grace to look uncomfortable: 'I have my sources,' he mumbled.

'I'm sure you do,' she teased, knowing exactly which agency provided her father's detailed information about the people she met. At first she had been angry to discover this prying into her life, had intended telling him exactly what she thought of his watchdog attitude, then she had realised he was only trying to protect her from other crooks like Rex. In the six months since she had found that first report amongst her father's papers in his study she had never once revealed that she knew of them. She had nothing to hide in her life, not from her father or anyone else, but this way she was assured that if anyone else did he would find out about it. What he had discovered about Jordan had just rekindled an almost dead interest, for she had felt until this time that Jordan had singled her out for his cruelty. Now it appeared that wasn't true, and knowing the reason for his cold ruthlessness made it easier to accept. Everyone had to have a weak spot; she intended being Jordan's. 'But haven't your sources told you that Jordan is still seeing Cathy, and that I—'

'Have seen a succession of men who mean nothing to you,' he sighed acknowledgement of the fact. 'You're almost twenty-one, Lara, it's time you settled down. On your birthday you'll inherit twenty per cent of the shares of Schofield Hotels,' he reminded her.

'And I'll continue to let you control them,' she said in a bored voice. 'As you have since you first made that provision for me. What do I know about the world of business?'

'You could learn—'

'No, I couldn't,' she gave a lightly dismissive laugh. 'Because I don't want to. I enjoy my life too much as it is to want to complicate it with business!'

'Then maybe you should find yourself a man of your own who can take care of it for you.'

'I already have.' She stood up with a grin. 'You!'

'I think I deserved that,' her father sighed defeat, watching as she pulled the short velvet cape about her shoulders, the same soft cream colour as her dress. 'You look beautiful, darling,' he told her with admiration.

'Thank you,' she smiled, freeing her hair from the collar of her cape to release it down her back.

'Who is the lucky man tonight?' he asked dryly.

'I haven't decided yet.' She laughed softly as he frowned. 'I'm going to a party, Daddy. I suppose the usual crowd will be there.'

'Including Jordan?'

Lara turned to the mirror to check her hair. 'I haven't

heard that his affair with Cathy is over,' she replied casually.

'Meaning he will be there.'

'Probably. Would you like to come? It's only at Basil's.'

Her father grimaced. Basil Jones was an extrovert of the first degree, and his parties usually bordered on the wild. 'Take care, darling,' he warned softly. 'Basil has been stalking you for months.'

She gave a husky laugh. 'But he isn't going to catch me!'

'Dozens of women all over the world would testify to claiming the same—before Basil got to work on them.'

'I can handle Basil,' she scorned, having become an expert at evading the biggest rake in London's rather obvious advances. Basil Jones was just another Gary Ridgeway, except perhaps with more style. But in his late thirties, like Gary, he was also too old for her tastes; she was not usually attracted to the rather obvious sophisticates of life, the men who considered every woman a mere conquest, who wouldn't remember the face of that woman a month after sharing her bed, let alone her name! Lara had become adept at avoiding such men, and so far Basil had seemed to accept her lighthearted refusals to his private invitations.

'I don't doubt it,' her father drawled. 'You're going to the party alone, then?'

She smiled teasingly. 'It isn't unheard of in the enlightened eighties.'

'No,' he sighed. 'Well, have a good time.'

Lara hesitated at the lounge door. Her father suddenly looked a lonely figure, with a sadness about him today that she couldn't explain. 'Are you sure you wouldn't like to come with me?' she offered softly, frowning her concern.

'Very sure.' He seemed to shake himself out of his mood of despondency. 'I seem to have been thinking about Marion a lot today, for some reason,' he explained as she continued to look concerned.

'I'll stay at home with you—'

'Certainly not!' He stood up. 'I have some work to do this evening, anyway.'

She didn't argue with him further, knowing by the determination in her father's face that he wanted to be alone. She respected the deep loss he felt for Marion, knew that by tomorrow he would probably be his old self again, that haunted look banished from his eyes.

Basil's party was well under way by the time she arrived shortly after ten, accepting her host's effusive compliments for exactly what they were, pure flattery.

'You're the most beautiful woman in London.' He kissed her fingertips, his Latin-dark eyes fixed on her glistening lips, the deep red lip-gloss emphasising their fullness. 'Absolutely beautiful, darling,' he murmured close to her earlobe as he himself removed her cape, unashamedly looking down at the bared fullness of her breasts above the strapless lace gown, the sheerness of the bodice not allowing for a bra to be worn beneath it.

'Thank you, Basil,' she dismissed, turning away to look for the familiar silver-blond head, having no interest at all in the rakishly-attractive dark-haired man at her side. She couldn't see Jordan in the crowded room, and turned to Basil with raised brows. 'Is everyone here?'

'Who knows, sweetie?' He gave an affected shrug, he was almost six feet in height, with a dark complexion and colouring that he said he owed to some equally rakish Spanish ancestor. Lara was inclined to think that ancestor had been with the Inquisition! 'I don't keep numbers, although it looks pretty crowded to me.' His arm was about her wrist as he held her against his side. 'Are you looking for anyone in particular?' His voice sharpened with interest.

'Not really.' She moved away from him. 'This party just doesn't seem to have your usual—style,' she drawled.

Basil flushed his displeasure, although he recovered quickly, smiling seconds later. 'Maybe we can have our own private party later, darling?' he said suggestively.

'I doubt it,' she drawled. 'Is Cathy here?' she asked with forced casualness. 'I have something I want to ask her,' she invented.

'Not yet,' he shook his head. 'Although it's still early. Grab yourself a drink, sweet,' he told her as a waiter moved towards them with a tray of glasses of champagne. 'And I'll get back to you. That's a promise,' he added suggestively.

It sounded more like a threat to her, but she wandered off to join a crowd of her friends, all the time keeping watch for the arrival of Cathy and Jordan.

When Cathy finally arrived shortly before twelve it wasn't with Jordan!

Lara almost choked on her champagne as she saw the young Adonis Cathy was clinging to as if he were truly a Greek god. Jordan might have been several years younger than the other woman, but this boy looked no older than Lara!

And where was Jordan? The relationship with Cathy was obviously over at last, but did that mean Jordan would disappear from the London social scene as suddenly as he had arrived? Heavens, she hoped not—she didn't even know his telephone number!

'This is Derek,' Cathy purred as Lara wandered casually over to greet her. 'He's in that new fabulous musical at the National.'

In it, but Lara doubted he had much of a part; Derek, she learnt over the next few minutes' conversation, had the body of Apollo and the brain of a fool. How Cathy could replace Jordan with him she just didn't know.

'No Jordan tonight?' she queried lightly once Cathy had stopped naming Derek's good qualities—all of which really meant he was good in bed! Lara had heard of actresses sleeping their way to the top, but this was ridiculous!

Cathy's mouth twisted. 'Don't be obtuse, darling. Jordan and I are no longer—together.' She looked up at Derek with hungry eyes.

Lara moistened her lips with the tip of her tongue. 'But he is still in London?'

'How should I know?' the other woman dismissed irritably. 'Yes, I suppose he is. Why should you be interested in Jordan's whereabouts?' she asked sharply.

'I'm not,' Lara replied coolly. 'My father played golf with him today, and he left his wallet at the club. I wondered—do you have his telephone number?'

'I do, but—Why not talk to the man face to face?' Cathy drawled with relish. 'He's just arrived.'

Lara turned slowly, her heart sinking as she saw the tiny blonde clinging to Jordan's arm. He hadn't wasted any time in replacing Cathy either. She hadn't even had the chance to become that replacement herself!

'Thanks,' she murmured distractedly to the Derek-engrossed Cathy, and made her way determinedly towards Jordan. Surely his little companion hadn't had a chance to become too firmly ensconced in his life; after all, he had been with Cathy until two evenings ago.

'Darling!' Basil greeted her throatily as she joined the group near the doorway. 'How nice, you came looking for me!'

She was too intent on the way Jordan looked to notice

Basil's warm embrace, the intimate smile he gave
her. Jordan's dark suit emphasised the breadth of his
shoulders, his skin looking darker than ever against the
white shirt. He was breathtaking, and she couldn't take
her eyes off him.

'Jordan,' she greeted him huskily.

Cool blue eyes were turned on her, his brows slightly
raised. 'Miss Schofield,' he returned abruptly.

Her mouth curved into a seductive smile. 'Surely we
don't need to be so formal?'

'Don't we?'

'No.' Her gaze met his in challenge. 'My father enjoyed his game of golf with you today.'

'He plays well,' he nodded.

'So do you, apparently,' she drawled, still not really
conscious of Basil's arm about her waist, his hand
dangerously close to her breast, aware only of Jordan
and her conversation with him. 'Does Miss—er—Do
you play golf?' she asked the tiny blonde girl haughtily.

'My name is Jennie Wright,' the other girl told her
distantly, she was in her late twenties at least. 'And golf
isn't a game that interests me.'

Lara could well imagine what games did! So far
Jordan's interest in women seemed to be in older, petite
women, certainly not a good omen for her. Maybe he
really *didn't* like tall, black-haired girls of twenty.

'If you'll excuse us . . .' Jordan said hardly.

'But—'

'I'm so glad you came looking for me, sweet,' Basil
leered at her as the other couple moved further into the
apartment, and for the first time Lara became aware of
how tightly he was holding her, his hand caressing
dangerously close to her breast now. 'Maybe we could
go off for that private party now?' he purred. 'Everyone
else seems to be happily—engaged.'

'No, I don't think so.' This time it wasn't so easy to extricate herself. 'Let go of me, Basil,' she ordered coldly.

The dark brown eyes flashed angrily. 'For God's sake stop being such a prude, darling! Larry Havers assures me it's all a veneer.'

'He *what*?' she exploded, suddenly still in his arms, breathing heavily from the exertion of trying to escape him. She had been out with Larry Havers just once, over a week ago, and she had treated him as coolly as all the other men she dated.

'Oh, come on, Lara,' Basil smiled encouragingly. 'No need to be so outraged. Larry didn't mean anything by it, and you know how men talk between themselves.'

'That's all they do as far as *I'm* concerned,' she snapped. 'What exactly did Larry tell you?'

'Oh, not the details, sweet. But he did say you're good,' he murmured close to her ear. 'Very good. But then I knew that, it isn't exactly a secret, is it?'

'It would seem not,' she said tightly, more outraged than she could ever remember being before. She couldn't believe the conceit of men, the absolute arrogance! One date with a man, possibly two, and a man's pride dictated that he had to claim a physical relationship with a woman. Well, Basil was one man who wouldn't be making that claim tomorrow, not with her anyway! 'Let me go, Basil,' she bit out contemptuously.

His eyes widened with a fury that she wouldn't have believed possible beneath the usual easygoing charm he displayed. And the way he was twisting her arm behind her back wasn't in her imagination either!

'Basil!' she gasped, unable to believe this could be happening to her. 'You're hurting me!'

'Walk!' he ordered tautly. 'My bedroom is through there,' he nodded in the direction of a slightly ajar door.

'I'm not going—'

'Please don't be difficult, darling,' he said in a mildly pleasant tone, only the glitter of his eyes telling her how dangerous his mood was. 'Almost everyone here is high on something,' he scorned, 'so no one is going to give a damn if we disappear into my bedroom for an hour or so.'

Lara cared! She had never been so scared in her life before. And Basil was right, everyone they passed seemed to ignore her pleas for help, their excited behaviour and loud talk indicating that they were indeed high on 'something'. And she had a feeling Basil was too. He was usually too lazy to exert himself in any way, and physical force didn't seem his way at all. It was just her luck that he should be this way tonight!

His bedroom had to be the height of eroticism, with mirrors on three of the walls and the ceiling, the round bed dominating most of the room, its velvet coverlet a deep chocolate brown, the bedroom furniture very ornate for a man's room.

Lara turned to face Basil as he finally released her arm. 'This is ridiculous—'

'I couldn't agree more, darling,' he drawled, pulling off his bow-tie. 'But if you want to play games . . .' he shrugged his acceptance.

'Games?' she frowned.

'Hard to get, sweetie,' he grinned, throwing off his jacket. 'Usually I find all that rough stuff a bit of a bore, but for a nubile young nymph like you I'm willing to make the exception.'

'But, Basil, I don't want—'

'I'm not ready to start the game yet, darling,' he laughed, his handsome face flushed with excitement. 'I want to shower first. Like to join me, we could begin our game in there?'

'No . . .'

'Shan't be long, sweetie.' He moved into the adjoining bathroom. 'Why don't you pour us a couple of drinks while you're waiting?' he unbuttoned his shirt. 'The bar is here.' He pressed a button and the top of the long dressing-table opening automatically, a drinks bar moving up within easy reach. 'Make mine a whisky and soda,' came his parting comment.

For a few dazed minutes Lara stared at the closed bathroom door, hearing the water being turned on, Basil actually singing softly to himself as he anticipated the next hour or so spent in bed with her. He really thought she was just going to stand here and wait for him! All this was a game to him, a bedroom game he thought she was participating in, willingly.

In her haste to escape from the bedroom she was looking behind her as she escaped, and walked straight into the solid wall of a muscular chest. 'I'm sorry! I—Jordan,' she breathed her relief as she looked up into navy blue eyes, clinging to the broad chest in front of her. 'Oh, Jordan, I—'

'What's the matter, Miss Schofield?' His narrowed gaze took in the mood of seduction in the room behind her, his mouth twisting with contempt for the obvious, as well as less obvious, effects designed to charm any woman into the luxury of the huge round bed, the alcohol obviously waiting to be consumed, the lighting soft and intimate, music playing softly in the almost soundproof room. 'Changed your mind about this one?' His gaze raked over her scornfully.

'You don't understand—'

'Oh, I think I do. The way Basil was touching you earlier it was obvious what the two of you had planned for tonight. Basil has more experience than even you,' he derided tauntingly. 'I'm sure you must have a lot to show each other.'

Lara had paled at his open-contempt for her. 'I only came here tonight to see you—'

'Me?' His dark blond brows rose. 'Why on earth should you want to see me?'

She flushed now. 'You know why,' she muttered, evading his gaze.

'Perhaps,' he nodded disdainfully. 'Subtlety is a word I would never use in connection with you,' he added with cruel mockery. 'Pick out the man you want and go for him, that seems to be your code of life. Unfortunately, this man isn't interested, and he never will be.' Once again he looked past her into the bedroom. 'Basil appears to be ready for you now,' he drawled.

Lara turned to find a puzzled Basil just emerging from the bathroom, his only clothing a dark brown bathrobe. He looked more than a little annoyed to see her standing in the open doorway with another man.

'I had no idea you didn't intend this to be strictly private, Lara,' he taunted as he joined them. 'No one mentioned you were into—'

'Basil, I don't think you understand.' Unknowingly her hands tightened on the lapels of Jordan's jacket, a look of panic widening her eyes.

'But of course I do, sweetie,' he gave her a suggestive smile. 'I'm only sorry I was so slow to understand.'

'No!' She evaded his hands as he would have reached for her. 'Please—'

'I think what Lara is trying to say,' surprisingly it was Jordan who came to her rescue, 'is that she's changed her mind.'

The older man's face darkened as he looked at them both, his mouth tightening ominously as he realised his victim was about to escape him.

'She's coming with me,' Jordan confirmed his suspic-

ions, his hold on her arm looking possessive. 'Aren't
you?' he prompted hardly, looking down at her.

'Er—yes.' Lara swallowed hard, never thinking he
would help her in this way after the insults he had made
about her morals a few minutes ago. 'I'm leaving with
Jordan,' she told Basil unhesitantly.

He gave an angry mutter before slamming the bedroom door in their faces.

'Always the gracious host,' Jordan mocked. 'This
party is turning into a damned orgy,' he muttered as a
couple pushed past them into the bedroom next to
Basil's, other couples not even bothering with such
privacy for their intimate caresses. 'You really want
to leave?' He looked down his long straight nose at
her.

'Yes,' she agreed eagerly.

'I'll just find Jennie.' His eyes were narrowed as he
scanned the entwined couples for the small blonde girl
who had arrived with him.

'Oh.'

His expression was mocking as he looked down at
Lara. 'Like I said, subtlety isn't a word that comes to
mind when I think of you.'

'And do you think of me?' she asked huskily.

'Not very often,' he replied with cold dismissal. 'Ah, I
see Jennie,' a smile lightened his harsh features. 'If you
want a lift home wait outside for us,' he instructed curtly.

'I came in my own car,' Lara felt forced to admit.

'Then there's nothing to stop you leaving, is there?'

'Jordan . . .'

'Yes?' he answered impatiently.

She frowned. 'Why don't you like me?'

'I don't?' he drawled.

She flushed at his mockery. 'You know you don't.'

'You're wrong,' he told her in mild tones. 'But has no

one ever told you the man likes to be the one doing the chasing?'

'I'll be an old woman by the time you get around to noticing me!' she snapped.

To her surprise—and delight—he began to laugh softly, his eyes deepening in colour, his teeth very white against his tanned skin. 'Haven't you noticed?' he taunted. 'I prefer my women to be older?'

'I can't wait that long,' she said moodily.

'You may have to,' he drawled.

Her eyes flashed deeply grey. 'You're enjoying this, damn you! Maybe I will join Basil after all,' she added rebelliously.

Jordan shrugged. 'Go ahead.'

Tears glistened in her eyes as she looked up at him. 'Don't you care?'

'Don't you?' he scorned. 'Look, Lara, it's your body. You don't seem to have been too discriminating who you gave it to in the past.'

'What do you mean?' she gasped, paling.

'You should have known when a man slept with you only to assess and steal your jewellery to be more careful who you take as a lover in future,' he derided. 'If the way you've been throwing yourself at me, a complete stranger, is anything to go by, you learnt nothing from that experience!'

Lara was appalled that he should know so much about her. He had only been in town a couple of months, but already he knew of her humiliation over Rex Maynard! But he had no right to talk to her so contemptuously, he couldn't possibly know the true facts. And after the things he had said to her she wasn't going to tell him either!

'I know more about *you* than you realise,' she told him defiantly.

His eyes narrowed, his mouth tightening as he became suddenly still. 'Indeed?' he rasped.

'Since Rex,' —even saying his name made her feel angry!—'my father has made a point of having all the people we come into contact with investigated.'

Was it her imagination, or did Jordan seem to tense even more? What could he possibly be afraid of anyone learning about him? Perhaps he was ashamed of his childhood, his adoption; he was certainly a cultured and well-spoken man now.

'I'm sure you must keep those investigators very busy with your numerous lovers,' he bit out insultingly before walking away.

Lara watched in dismay as he joined Jennie, his arm about the girl's waist as they left a few seconds later, Jordan not sparing Lara so much as a second glance.

Well, she hadn't handled that very well. All that had happened had been that they had ended up trading insults. And she had intended being so understanding, to have Jordan become attracted to her in spite of his animosity. All she had succeeded in doing tonight had been to alienate him further. He hadn't liked the idea of being investigated at all, had seemed really angered by it. Granted, what her father had found out about him had pointed to a checkered childhood and early manhood, but that had been something he had no control over at the time. He had managed to make a success of his life despite that.

'Changed your mind again, Lara?' purred a deeply familiar voice from behind her.

She spun round to find Basil leaving his bedroom, fully dressed again now. 'Don't you ever give up?' she snapped, taking both her anger at him personally, and Jordan, out on him.

'Never, sweetie,' his good humour seemed restored.

'*Have* you changed your mind?' he repeated hopefully.

'No!' she bit out.

'Pity,' he drawled. 'Oh well, I suppose I'd better find a woman who is willing. It wouldn't do for me, as the host, not to make some lucky woman happy for the night.'

Lara gave a snort of disgust, and spun on her heel to leave, and her last sight of Basil was of him approaching a leggy redhead.

She was beginning to tire of this constant party scene, of the meaningless relationships that went on about her. She just hadn't found anything better to replace it yet.

It was through choice that Lara stayed in more often than usual during the next two weeks, her disgust with Basil and the crowd she usually mixed with persisting. She no longer felt at ease with such people now that she knew they believed her to be as promiscuous as themselves, and whereas before she had willingly joined in the ripping of someone's character to shreds, she now wondered what was said about *her* when she wasn't around. Basil had given her an insight into the men's boastful conversations about her, and she could well imagine the bitchiness that circulated among the women.

She saw nothing of Jordan Sinclair, spending what evenings she did go out with the quietly respectable Nigel. Those evenings told her that he still wasn't the man for her, that a man with silver-blond hair and navy-blue eyes still haunted her dreams, as elusive then as he was in reality.

'Like to come to the club?' her father offered as she moped around the house one Saturday afternoon. 'I feel like a round of golf, and the fresh air would probably do you good,' he frowned at the lack of colour in her cheeks. 'I've been very worried about you lately.'

'Because I'm staying in?' she mocked lightly. 'Most parents would worry because I was out too much!'

'I did,' he nodded. 'But now I'm worrying because this staying at home isn't like you. Did anything happen at Basil's party that I should know about?'

'Not a thing,' she dismissed evasively. 'And I'll give golf a miss for today if you don't mind, Nigel is coming over later. Do you have someone you could have a round with?'

He shrugged. 'There's always someone at the club willing for a game.'

'Has Jordan Sinclair beaten you lately?' Lara asked the question casually, hoping her father wouldn't realise how interested she was in the answer.

'Not lately,' he shook his head. 'He's not been to the club the last few weeks.'

That didn't please her at all. She had to admit, to herself at least, that another reason she had absented herself from the usual round of parties had been because she hoped Jordan would miss her presence. She knew he had played golf with her father two weeks ago, that he was now a member of the club; if he had been away on business then he wouldn't have been around to notice her own absence. Damn!

'I'll see you later, love,' her father ruffled her hair affectionately before leaving.

Her mind was only half on her actions as she prepared for her date with Nigel, her heart not really in it. Nigel was becoming more and more persistent about her meeting his parents, and the more she saw of him the more averse she became to the idea. Maybe the parties and the meaningless people she met at them were a bore, but she wasn't sure how much more of Nigel's undivided attention she could take.

He didn't complain once later that afternoon as she

dragged him around endless shops, not really buying anything, but spending hours just looking. Lara decided he was going to make someone a very docile husband one day—but not her! She had tried things her father's way, had tried to 'settle down' with Nigel, but if she became any more bored with him she was going to fall asleep in his company. She regretted having already agreed to have dinner with him tonight now, knew that after tonight she couldn't see him again.

Her father still hadn't returned from the club when she came home to change for dinner, and so she decided he must be dining out himself tonight.

Her dress was a knee-length black lace, the sheerness of the bodice with its darker flower shadings over her bare breasts leaving very little to the imagination. She looked beautifully seductive, and it seemed a shame it was all to be wasted on Nigel.

Not that he seemed to consider it wasted when he arrived shortly after seven, only waiting long enough for the maid to depart before taking her in his arms, 'Darling, you look sensational!' he told her raggedly.

Lara turned away from his obvious intention to kiss her. 'My lip-gloss,' she reminded him waspishly, having no interest in letting him kiss her.

He laughed softly. 'You can always put some more on.' He kissed her lightly on the lips, savouring the moment. 'Mm, darling, you taste delicious!' Before Lara could even guess at his intent he took her lips in a devouring kiss that robbed her body of all its breath.

She hadn't believed nice dependable Nigel was capable of such savagery, and her head bent back as she lay helpless in his arms.

'Darling Lara,' he groaned against her throat, his hands caressing her body with fevered excitement. 'Oh, darling!' The shudder of his body told her he was near to being out of control.

'Nigel—'

'Let's stay here,' he encouraged heatedly, urging her back towards the sofa, quickly joining her on its long length as she overbalanced on to it. 'Your father is out, and no one will disturb us. Oh, Lara!' once again he began to kiss her.

'. . . and as I told—Lara!' It was the scandalised tone of her father's voice that finally persuaded Nigel to release her. 'I—I—Good God!' he groaned in an embarrassed voice.

With a look that shot venom at Nigel, Lara turned to explain the situation to her father—only to find he wasn't alone. Standing a short distance behind him, his navy blue eyes filled with contempt, was Jordan Sinclair.

CHAPTER THREE

IT was the second time in just over two weeks that Jordan Sinclair had caught her in a compromising position, and she knew his contempt was deserved.

Her father looked more embarrassed than anything, and with a growing blush of confusion Lara stood up, brushing down the chiffon skirt of her black dress.

'I'm sorry about that, sir—er—Mr Schofield.' Amazingly Nigel was the first to speak, standing at her side now, his dark hair ruffled to disorder. 'Lara looks so beautiful that—Well, I'm sure you understand,' he gave a sheepish smile.

Her father was fast regaining his composure, coming fully into the lounge now, Jordan slowly following him. 'Lara is a grown woman,' he accepted. 'And you did think you were alone.'

'Thank you, sir.' Nigel gave a pleased smile that his apology had been accepted so readily.

Lara was still most aware of the silent contempt of Jordan Sinclair, knew that most of her father's embarrassment had been caused because this man had also been a witness to the passionate little scene. Lara also wished it had been anyone but him who had walked in with her father. With a lot of her father's friends she could have laughed off this situation, but with the scene with Basil also against her in Jordan's eyes there was no way she could banish the impression he must have gained of her by now of being a little tease. Besides, if the grapevine had told him about Rex then he must also

47

have heard the lying boasts of the men she had dated in the past.

'Sorry, darling.' Her father kissed her lightly on the cheek, his eyes regretful. 'I've brought Jordan back for dinner,' he informed her with forced cheerfulness, telling her that his embarrassment was still with him.

'So I can see,' she returned just as lightly. 'Did you defeat my father at golf once again, Mr Sinclair?' she enquired coolly, determined not to feel uncomfortable in his presence, despite her flushed appearance and her lack of lip-gloss.

He seemed amused that she should be the one to revert to the formal this evening. 'As a matter of fact,' he drawled, 'it was your father's turn to win today.'

'Really?' Her eyes widened with surprise. 'How clever of you, Daddy,' she smiled at him, her eyes averted from the blatant masculinity of a hardly muscled chest beneath a black roll-necked sweater, the grey cords moulded to the long length of lean legs. The golden-silver hair had been tousled by the brisk April wind, giving Jordan a rakish appearance he didn't even seem aware of. But Lara was aware of everything about him, and after his cruel dismissal of her the last time they had met she felt angry with herself for still feeling this attraction for him.

Her father looked pleased by her praise. 'I think Jordan is just tired after his business trip to Germany,' he modestly excused.

She turned cool grey eyes to the other man. 'You've been away?'

He nodded abruptly. 'That's right. Although from what your father has been telling me I haven't missed much. No party could ever hope to be a success without the lovely Lara Schofield in attendance!'

Lara deliberately put her hand in the crook of Nigel's

arm, moving closer to him. It would seem her father had mentioned her lack of interest in the usual round of parties to Jordan, although Jordan didn't seem to have mentioned the embarrassing scene that had caused her aversion. For that, at least, she felt grateful. Although it still didn't erase her antagonism towards him. 'Nigel and I have been getting to know each other better,' she told him softly. 'That's so difficult to do at a party.'

'I agree.' Jordan held her gaze for long, breathless minutes. 'I hope we didn't interrupt this "getting to know each other better" just now?' he drawled.

Lara flushed—as she was sure she was intended to. And the uncomfortable look seemed to be back in her father's face too. 'You didn't,' she told Jordan abruptly. 'Nigel and I are just on our way out now,' she said tautly. 'We have a table booked for dinner.'

'Then we mustn't keep you,' he mocked.

She kissed her father goodbye under the mocking view of those navy blue eyes as Jordan made himself comfortable in an armchair, making it obvious that her presence wasn't required for him to have a pleasant evening at her home. In fact, she felt sure he would enjoy himself more once she had gone!

She felt angry and frustrated by the fact that Jordan was at her home and she had to spend the evening with Nigel, becoming more and more so as the evening wore on. Nigel annoyed her as never before, until in the end she couldn't stop herself snapping at him.

'Darling . . . ?' He seemed totally bewildered by her strange behaviour tonight.

'Don't call me that!' she glared across the table at him.

'It's just a term of affection—'

'That's exactly it!' she snapped again. 'Who asked you to feel affection for me?' All her anger towards Jordan Sinclair bubbled over at the unsuspecting Nigel.

'Lara—'

'We've been out together a few times and you act as if you own me!' She threw her serviette on to the table and picked up her clutch-bag.

'I want to marry you—'

'And I *don't* want to marry you!' She stood up. 'I'd like to leave now.'

'But—'

'*Now!* Nigel.' She glared down at him with tightlipped anger.

Poor Nigel looked even more bewildered, shooting her puzzled glances as he settled the bill for their dinner.

By the time they got outside Lara had had time to be deeply ashamed of her behaviour, never having been so cruel to another human being before. Nigel looked so hurt still, and she wished she could tell him that it had all been a mistake, that she really did love him. But however cruelly the words had been spoken, they had told him the truth—she didn't want him to love her, and she didn't want to marry him.

She had been such a bitch, her words designed to hurt—as she knew they had. But if she apologised now, if she told him she hadn't meant it, she had a feeling that Nigel would once again give her that dog-like devotion that she found so stifling. And so despite the hurt and confusion she saw in the pained brown eyes, she didn't say a word on the drive back to her home.

'Don't say anything, Nigel,' she warned him as she got out of the car, her eyes flashing.

'But—'

'It's over,' she told him abruptly.

'But—'

She didn't wait to hear any more, but turned to enter her home, using her key, seeing no point in putting someone to the trouble of opening the door for her when she could easily let herself in.

Besides, she didn't want to see anyone just yet, she still felt awful about the way she had finished things with Nigel. What was the saying, 'being cruel to be kind'? Yes, she had been cruel, but had it been kind? Probably. Nigel had been hanging around her for months, and until the last two weeks she hadn't encouraged him to think he was anything special to her; only the truth would put him off now, she knew that.

She had forgotten Jordan Sinclair was dining with her father until she walked into the lounge and saw him relaxing on the sofa, a glass of brandy swirling idly between the long fingers of his right hand. She came to a halt just inside the room as she saw the curtains hadn't been pulled across the window, that this room looked directly out to the front of the house. Had he seen—?

'Yes,' he murmured softly as her wide-eyed gaze returned to the sun-bronzed face, 'I saw. What did you do to the poor boy? He looked quite stricken,' he taunted.

Lara flicked her hair back over her shoulder with a defiant gesture. 'Where's my father?'

'In his study, taking an overseas call,' Jordan drawled. 'You didn't tell me what you've done to poor Wentworth.'

Her eyes flashed as she strolled confidently into the room. 'That's because it's none of your business,' she snapped.

'No?' He arched dark blond brows.

'No!' She moved agitatedly to the drinks tray on the side-cabinet and poured herself a large measure of gin, adding only a small amount of tonic to it, spilling some of it over her hand as she turned to find Jordan standing dangerously close behind her. She looked up at him with wide eyes, her lashes fluttering nervously.

'I don't think your father would approve of that,' he nodded down at the glass full of alcohol she clutched on to. 'He seems concerned about you.'

Lara flushed. 'I can't imagine why.'

'Can't you?' he mocked.

Her mouth firmed. 'No.'

'Is Wentworth out of the picture now?'

'I don't see that—'

'Is he?' Jordan bit out in a rasping voice.

Her rebellion died a swift death as she recognised a will far stronger than her own. 'I hope so,' she admitted tightly.

'And Basil?'

'Was never in it,' she scorned.

'Gary?'

'Not him, either. Look, Mr Sinclair—'

'Don't be ridiculous, Lara,' he taunted. 'You know damn well you haven't thought of me as "Mr Sinclair" since the first moment we met.'

His voice had lowered seductively, and she raised questioning eyes to his narrowed ones. 'Have I suddenly got older?' she queried softly.

Jordan gave a laugh of throaty enjoyment. 'You could say that,' his gaze was caressing on her puzzled face. 'I just wanted to make sure all your other lovers were out of the picture.' He sobered suddenly. 'I'm one of that peculiar breed of men who like to think they're the only man in a woman's life. Your father has given me permission to ask you out to dinner tomorrow—will you come?' He looked at her with challenge.

'You *asked my father*?' she gasped.

He nodded. 'I had the impression he didn't quite trust me where his only child is concerned—you are an only child, aren't you?' His eyes were narrowed.

'Yes. But—'

'Thank God for that,' he grimaced. 'Two like you would be too much!'

Lara frowned, ignoring the taunt for the moment. 'Let me get this straight,' she said slowly. 'You asked my father if you could take me out and he said yes?'

'That's right,' Jordan taunted. 'Surprised?'

'Very,' she said dryly.

'I think he was pleased that I'd bothered to ask him.'

'Why did you?' She gave him a probing look.

'You don't want to have dinner with me?'

She flushed. 'That isn't the point. And no, I'm not sure that I do,' she added moodily. 'I don't understand my father agreeing either, I could have sworn you were Number One on his list of dangerous young men.'

Jordan shrugged. 'He must have changed his mind about me.'

'As you seem to have done about me,' she said thoughtfully. 'Unless, of course, you've been listening to the same rubbishy gossip Basil has.' Her eyes flashed angrily. 'I never realised until he told me what was said about me how you men need to protect your ego. Contrary to what he, and everyone else in that crowd, thinks, I do not sleep around. And if you're inviting me out with the sole intention of going to bed with me then you're going to be as disappointed as all those other would-be-lovers,' she added the last scornfully.

One lean hand moved up to gently caress her face. 'Am I?'

His fingers against her cheek were working magic with her senses, and she felt herself sway towards him. 'I—'

Jordan bent his head, his mouth briefly claiming hers. But it was enough to silence any protest Lara might even have been thinking of making. And she wasn't sure she had been going to make any!

'I'll call for you at seven-thirty tomorrow.' His smile was quietly triumphant as he moved away from her, her expression dazed.

'Sorry to have—You're back early, Lara,' her father frowned as he came through from his study, his narrowed gaze on Jordan's arm as it still curved about his daughter's waist. 'Where's Nigel?' he asked abruptly.

'Er—'

'Luckily for me they—had a disagreement,' Jordan drawled as she seemed to be having trouble answering.

'Indeed?' Her father's frown deepened.

'I think I should be going now,' Jordan said briskly. 'I had a nice evening, Joseph. We must do it again some time. Walk me to the door, Lara?' he quirked dark blond brows at her questioningly.

Considering she was a girl who hated to be managed, Jordan Sinclair was doing a good job of doing exactly that! She had never before been out on a date with one man and ended the evening by being kissed goodnight by another one. She had never been quite so dazed by a kiss before either. What *was* it about this man that affected her in quite this way, why did he—

'Lara?' he prompted hardly.

'I—Oh yes,' she gave her father an uncertain look before leading the way out to the spacious hallway. 'Jordan, I—' Once again it was his mouth on hers that stopped her words of protest, and there was nothing light about this kiss, his lips plundered hers with ruthless determination.

Lara felt dizzy, clinging to him weakly, feeling the strength and power in the width of his shoulders beneath her hands, looking up at him with wide eyes as he at last held her at arm's length.

'Seven-thirty,' he reminded her softly before leaving.

It took her several minutes to collect her thoughts

together enough to rejoin her father in the lounge. Why Jordan had changed his mind about her she didn't know; she just knew she was glad he had. She was more than ever convinced she had never known a man like him before, and—

'Daddy?' Her father was scowling heavily when she returned to the lounge. 'Is there something wrong?' she frowned her concern.

He gave her a disapproving look. 'Why didn't you tell me about the scene with Basil?'

Hot colour washed over her in waves. Only one person could possibly have told her father about Basil—

'Yes, Jordan told me,' her father rasped, throwing half the whisky in his glass to the back of his throat, swallowing it without even a wince. 'I felt a fool after my reaction to you kissing Nigel earlier, bumbled on about how pleased I was that you at last seemed to be settling down to seeing one man, told Jordan how worried I'd been about the crowd you'd been mixing with.' He fixed her with eyes as grey as her own, the similarity between them very noticeable in that moment. 'You can imagine how I felt when he then informed me of your presence in Basil's bedroom.'

'That was only—I didn't intend—'

'Didn't intend your teasing to go quite that far,' her father finished angrily.

'No! I—'

'I've watched the way you tease and test men, Lara,' his mouth twisted, 'and if Basil had forced the issue I couldn't have exactly blamed him.'

'It wasn't like that,' she insisted heatedly, furious with Jordan Sinclair more than with anyone else. How dared he tell her father about Basil! 'I had no idea he intended making love to me—'

'Don't be naïve, Lara,' he scowled, finishing off his

whisky. 'You've been a worry to me for years now with your flirtatious ways, but I thought you had enough sense not to get yourself into such a situation. I take it you didn't genuinely find the man attractive?' he derided.

'Basil? Of course not,' she scorned.

'And Nigel?'

She flushed. 'Now you're starting to sound like Jordan,' she snapped, unable to remember the last time her father had spoken to her in this way—if he ever had! She only ever remembered him being an indulgent and loving parent, couldn't remember him being this angry even over the Rex Maynard business.

'I'm very grateful for his help. If he hadn't—'

'Interference, you mean,' she bit out tautly. 'I handled that incident with Basil, Jordan had no need to even bother you with it.'

Her father's mouth was tight. 'As I understand it Jordan had a lot to do with "handling" Basil!'

'I could have managed without his help—'

'You shouldn't have had to manage anything,' her father's voice rose angrily. 'And what did you and Nigel argue about tonight?'

Lara turned away. 'We didn't argue—at least, not exactly. I just don't want to go out with him any more.'

'After stringing him along for months!' He gave a disgusted sigh. 'That was cruel, Lara. Maybe I've just never noticed before,' he shook his head, 'or maybe you haven't always been like this—I really hope not!—but I think you're a spoilt little brat. Men aren't toys to be played with, and discarded the moment they tire or bore you. I doubt you'll have the opportunity to play with Jordan, he's a—What did you say?' he demanded to know as Lara muttered something under her breath. 'Lara?' he prompted sharply.

'I said I've changed my mind about going out with him tomorrow night,' she revealed reluctantly, her eyes glittering furiously. 'I have no intention of going out with such a—'

'You'll go!' her father thundered—her dear, kind father who *never* lost his temper. 'It seems I've raised a pampered little madam,' he scowled. 'But if you've agreed to go out with the man then you'll go!'

They were both breathing hard as they glared at each other across the room. She and her father never, ever argued, and her father had never criticised her like this before either. It was all Jordan Sinclair's fault, damn him.

She took a deep controlling breath, going over to her father's side. 'Now don't be cross, darling,' she pouted up at him. 'I may have been a little naughty, but—'

'This method of placating me may have worked when you were in your early teens, Lara,' he derided dryly, 'but it certainly doesn't have the same effect now. You've told Jordan you'll go out with him, and even though he knows what a spoilt little brat you are he still wants to see you. You'll go,' he told her in a voice that brooked no argument.

'I thought you didn't like him,' she muttered moodily.

'I didn't say that, I said he could be dangerous, and I'm sure he can. But it seems you like danger, that it attracts you. At least Jordan is man enough to protect you.'

'And who's going to protect me from him!'

His mouth twisted. 'I didn't think you wanted protecting from him. At least he's a man, Lara, better than all these namby-pamby idiots you keep going out with. And at least he asked my permission before he asked you out, and that's more than any of your other men ever did!'

'This is the twentieth century—'

'And that means that all respect for the older generation has gone, I suppose?' he scorned. 'Marion would never have—God, why is she so much on my mind lately?' He looked at the photograph of the woman that had been his wife as it stood on the mantelpiece. 'I loved her, and I always feel as if she's with me, but just lately . . .' he gave a puzzled shake of his head. 'I find myself thinking of her at the strangest times,' he gave an impatient sigh. 'She wouldn't have liked your wild friends and the even wilder parties, Lara,' he spoke more gently now. 'I'm sorry I shouted at you, love,' he added softly, 'but this thing with Basil has unnerved me. What if he hadn't taken no for an answer? I know you like to act sophisticated, darling, but you aren't permissive like the crowd you run around with, and one of these days one of the men isn't going to take no as your final answer.'

'And if it's Jordan Sinclair?'

He shook his head with confidence. 'Jordan is ultimately a man who is in control. If a woman says no then he'll accept that.'

Lara moistened her lips. 'And if I find I don't want to say no?'

Her father met her gaze steadily. 'Then it will be your decision. I'm not a prude, Lara, and I doubt you are either. If you find a man you want to make love with then that's fine by me. But I don't want you to fall into the merry-go-round whirl of bed-sharing that goes on amongst Basil's crowd. I have enough confidence in you to know going to bed with a man will mean more to you than just a casual affair.'

Lara felt weary with exhaustion as she prepared for bed later that evening. She and her father were friends again, that wasn't what was troubling her. What did worry her was that although she should feel angry with

Jordan for the trouble he had caused tonight between her father and herself, *did* feel angry with him because of it, she still wanted to see him tomorrow night. And that had nothing to do with the fact that her father had decided she should. Jordan himself commanded her with an easy arrogance that he expected to be obeyed, successfully quietening any protests she might make to the contrary with the physical attraction she couldn't hide from him.

But if she felt that weakness towards him she was determined it wouldn't all be one-sided, dressing with a seduction of her own for her date with him the next evening. She had spent the afternoon at the hairdressers, her long hair pulled back severely from her face to a neat coil on top of her head, the severity of the style emphasising the clear lines of her face, the fine brows, the fascination of luminous grey eyes, highly defined cheekbones, a pert nose, her mouth a deep pout of copper-coloured seduction. The dress was new, virginal white, caught across one shoulder, with a low-hipped waistline that emphasised rather than hid the supple curves beneath, finishing silkily just below her knees, her legs long and slender, her feet thrust into delicate white evening sandals.

She felt and looked marvellous, and she was ready on time, although she deliberately kept Jordan waiting when he arrived at seven-forty. If he wanted to keep her waiting then she would return the gesture, so she deliberately lingered in her room.

'Your father had to leave for his own dinner engagement.' Jordan stood up as she came into the room, tall and lithe in a dark evening suit. 'I almost went with him,' he rasped. 'Do you realise it's eight o'clock?'

Lara arched black brows, making a point of looking at the tiny gold watch on her slender wrist. 'So it is.' Her lips curved into a smile, although her eyes remained hard, completely lacking in humour.

'Payment time?' he drawled.

'For what?' she returned smoothly.

'For my own unavoidable ten minutes' delay,' his mouth twisted. 'If you want to play childish games, mete out punishment for an urgent business matter that required my attention and meant I didn't get back to my apartment to change until seven o'clock—'

'Is that why you were late?'

He gave an angry sigh. 'As a matter of fact, yes. I suppose you considered it a personal slur on your desirability?' he derided hardly.

Lara flushed at the taunt. 'You know damn well your lateness has nothing to do with my anger! Well . . . not much, anyway,' she amended at his mocking look. 'I suppose it was too much trouble to pick up a telephone and tell me you'd been delayed?' she asked with saccharine sweetness.

'In this case, yes.' His mouth was tight.

She shot him an angry glare. 'What I'm really furious about is that you saw fit to interfere in my life and told my father about Basil. You had no right to do that!'

'Told his little girl off, did he?'

His mockery made her blush deepen. 'Mind your own damned business—'

'I can see he did,' Jordan mused. 'But someone had to stop you, you were on a roller-coaster to self-destruction, were mixing with a crowd where drugs and easy sex are readily available.'

'You were with the same crowd,' she reminded him heatedly, feeling about ten years old!

'I'm thirty years old,' he reasoned. 'I've been about a lot longer than you, seen life a lot tougher than you even dreamed about. The drugs I'm not interested in, the sex I take when I want it,' he shrugged.

'I noticed!' Lara derided.

His eyes flashed deeply navy blue. 'You have an air of reckless challenge about you that will one day tempt you to experiment with both the drugs and the sex.'

'But you're the one who's going to take me away from all that, right?' she scorned. 'I thought we were going out to dinner, not getting married!'

Jordan's eyes glazed over with an icy anger. 'The man who is foolish enough to marry you will have to be even more strong-willed than you are.'

'Like you?' she scoffed.

'Yes,' he bit out grimly.

She gave a gasp of indignation. 'Just because my father has decided you're the blue-eyed boy it doesn't mean I feel the same way,' she snapped.

To her chagrin Jordan smiled, not at all angered by her insulting behaviour. 'Men have a way of feeling like that when you protect their only daughters from a nasty seducer and they beat you at golf all in one day. The first speaks for itself, and the second—well, they feel sorry for you, as if they've really injured your pride. And then they try to make it up to you, in my case your father thought it would be a wonderful idea if I took you out '

'You let him win!' Lara slowly gasped as realisation dawned. 'You *let* my father win at golf on purpose!'

'Make you feel better?' he taunted. 'I lost a perfectly good round of golf so that I could take you out to dinner. Telling him about Basil clinched it as far as your father was concerned.'

'You devious—'

'Conniving, arrogant,' he finished lazily, as if the accusations had been levelled at him many times before.

'It gets results, though, doesn't it?' he raised dark blond brows.

Lara continued to look at him for a long speechless moment, overwhelmed by this man who was going to take her out for the evening. And then she began to laugh, to really enjoy the power Jordan had to manipulate people to his will, his design. Such a man was exciting to be around.

For a few moments he seemed surprised by her laughter, and then he joined in her humour, smiling ruefully. 'Let's go to dinner,' he suggested indulgently. 'I have a feeling it's going to be an interesting evening!'

Interesting was one of the things being with Jordan was; it was also nerve-tingling, exciting. Jordan had a way of giving her his full attention, of making her feel like the only woman that mattered to him in a room full of beautiful women.

'What happened to Jennie?' She looked at him beneath sooty lashes as they lingered on in the restaurant after their meal.

'Jennie?' he frowned.

'The woman you were with at Basil's party,' she reminded him irritably, wondering if he always forgot the women in his life this quickly once he had passed on to a new challenge.

'Ah, that Jennie,' he nodded. 'I was only looking after her for a friend.'

'How nice!'

His gaze sharpened at her sarcasm. 'Making sure she wasn't lonely,' he rasped, 'while her husband was away on business.'

'Even nicer!'

'Other men might find this brittle sophistication you display fascinating,' he snapped, 'but I don't!'

'Sorry!' she flushed.

Jordan gave an angry sigh. 'You aren't sorry at all. Ben Wright happens to be an old friend of mine, and Jennie is his wife. I do not have the slightest interest in married women,' he added harshly.

Her eyes widened at the vehemence behind the last statement. He really felt strongly about the subject. 'Have you ever been married?' she asked curiously.

He looked at her consideringly. 'Why do you want to know?'

'I just—wondered,' she shrugged.

His mouth twisted. 'No, I've never been married.'

'And don't intend to be either,' she derided dryly. 'It was just longing to be added to the end of that statement,' she explained at his raised brows.

'You're probably right,' he mused hardly. 'Marriage holds little appeal for me.'

It hadn't held much appeal for her either until she met Jordan. But she found him more exciting than any other man she had ever met, knew that he had so much depth of character that she would never feel boredom in his company. And most of all he was the biggest challenge of her young life, was a man she longed to bend to her will—and yet she knew she would never succeed; Jordan was a man who would always hold a lot of himself back. She hadn't questioned him directly about his past, but had known by his silence as she talked of her own happy childhood that his hadn't been as pleasant. She wanted desperately to be the one he opened up to, the one he told his innermost thoughts to. And for a girl who had basically had only her own interests at heart for most of her life that was some admission.

'I've had a lovely time,' she told him as they sat in his parked car outside her home. Jordan hadn't so much as made an effort to put his arm about her shoulders, let alone kiss her goodnight—and Lara wasn't moving until he did.

'Good,' came his abrupt answer.

'It was a nice restaurant.'

His mouth twisted with derision. 'I'm sure you've been there before.'

It was one of the most fashionable restaurants in town, and as she was a very fashion-conscious young lady it was obvious she would have been there in the past. 'Well— yes. But never with such scintillating company.'

'Thank you,' he gave an arrogant inclination of the silver-blond head in acknowledgement of the compliment.

But again he gave no indication of whether or not he had enjoyed the evening too, and Lara gave a frustrated sigh. Wasn't the man even going to kiss her goodnight? She felt sure he usually did a lot more than that with his woman, that most of the time he didn't say goodnight but good *morning*. Maybe that was the trouble, maybe he felt inhibited by the fact that she lived with her father.

'Would you like to come in for coffee?' she offered eagerly. 'Daddy's car isn't back, so he isn't home from the Major's yet.'

'The Major?' Jordan frowned. 'I somehow had the impression your father would be spending the evening with a woman.'

'Oh no,' she laughed. 'Daddy doesn't date. I'm afraid it would take someone very special to take the place of Marion, in either of our lives. She was a unique lady.'

'So I can see,' his voice sounded harsh. 'In that case, coffee sounds good.'

. All her acquired sophistication seemed to desert her when she was around this man, and it was only with supreme effort of will on her part that she stopped a ridiculous smile of pleasure crossing her face as she let them both into the house with her key, the housekeeper having gone to bed hours ago.

'Coffee and sandwiches are always left out for us in the kitchen,' Lara explained as Jordan took her wrap. 'I won't be long.'

'I'm not hungry.' His hands returned to her waist after throwing the wrap down carelessly on the hall chair. 'And I had coffee at the restaurant.'

Lara stared up at him with wide-eyed fascination, wondering at the pain and disillusionment that had put the lines beside his nose and mouth, making him seem much older than his thirty years. Jordan himself had told her he had seen a much tougher life than she, and it had left its mark on him. She put up a hand to smooth away those lines. 'Oh, Jordan,' she groaned weakly, her mouth raised invitingly to his.

The savage curve of his lips claimed possession of hers, parting their softness, his hands against her spine curving her body into his, crushing her breasts against the hardness of his chest, holding her hips firmly into his.

His hair felt thick and vibrant beneath her touch as she caressed his nape, his lips on her bare shoulder now, gently biting and kissing the soft flesh with an eroticism that made her legs tremble.

'Do we have to do our lovemaking out in the hallway?' he mocked softly.

Lara blushed, blinking to clear her befuddled brain. 'No, of course not.'

Jordan's arm about her waist guided her to the sofa in the lounge, his gaze holding hers as he laid her down on its length before slowly joining her.

'Jordan—'

'Yes?' He had released the single shoulder fastening of the dress now, no zips or catches to mar its simple design, her breasts bare beneath the silky material.

The first unfamiliar feel of a man's lips on her breasts caused a gasp of surprised pleasure to escape her lips, the nipples instantly hardening and straining forward so that they too could know the magic of a warm mouth and caressing tongue. But Jordan was in no hurry to claim them, kissing each creamy inch of her pert breasts, and Lara's deep groans of frustrated pleasure had no effect. As his tongue traced the outline of first one nipple and then the other she shuddered with a reaction that was out of her control, strong hands caressing down to her waist and hips, pushing her dress aside where it hindered his movement as he bit down gently on her taut breast.

Those strong hands lingered on the lacy top to her briefs, but the touch of Jordan's lips on hers had her lost in a sea of sensuous delight that didn't allow for speech, only gasps and groans of ecstasy as one of his hands found the centre of her passion, caressing her with soft gentle movements that had her arching against him in surrender.

Lara had never known such intimate lovemaking, had never allowed another man the freedom of her body that this man was taking as if it were his right. But the trembling in her limbs, the spiralling pleasure, told her that she couldn't stop it now, that she wanted to go on to the end, to know the ultimate pleasure this man could give her, that he was giving her now. None of the textbook lovemaking she had read about had warned her of the senses singing to the touch of a man's hand, of the ecstasy that couldn't be controlled beneath such expert caresses.

She blinked her bewilderment as Jordan moved back to straighten her dress, his face and hands absorbed in the task. 'Jordan . . . ?' she gasped her dismay.

'Not here, Lara.' He pushed the damp tendrils of her hair back behind her ears as they escaped the neat coil.

'Your father could come home at any moment, and we don't want a repeat of yesterday.' His mouth twisted.

She hadn't cared about her father as Jordan touched her, hadn't cared about anything but that the caresses continue to the dizzying end. Now she blushed, knowing that Jordan had been much less out of control than she had, that he might not even have been out of control at all. 'I was selfish,' she realised guiltily. 'I didn't touch or kiss you in return.'

'Maybe next time.' He stood up to straighten his jacket, his hair still ruffled from her first heated caresses.

Lara sat up too, still feeling shaken from a desire that had stopped just short of assuagement. 'Will there be a next time?' She moistened her lips, wanting so desperately to see him again, aching for him in the depths of her body.

Jordan's expression was hooded as he looked down at her, her eyes still glazed with passion, her lips bare of any colour but a natural one, the tender skin of her shoulders and breasts showing a faint redness from the slight roughness of his jaw. 'Dinner tomorrow?' he suggested softly. 'At my apartment?'

She swallowed hard. 'I—I'd like that,' she accepted both the dinner and his other unspoken, but understood, invitation.

CHAPTER FOUR

JORDAN's apartment was exactly what Lara had expected it to be, the lounge ultra-modern, the furniture very square and hard-looking, the colour scheme mainly brown and white, all the modern conveniences in the large kitchen where the cook had left everything prepared for their dinner before leaving, a candlelit table set for two in the adjoining dining-room.

Lara had been captivated the moment she saw Jordan again, all the self-doubt and surprise at her behaviour the previous evening melting away at the warmth of his eyes; the intimate setting in the apartment was ideal for her mood, their conversation was low and slightly breathless on her part; she felt a little like a child in love for the first time. She was far from being a child, although she was beginning to have the suspicion that she could be in love!

There could be no other explanation for the way she had seemed to float to bed the evening before, sleeping deeply and waking with a smile to her lips, filled with a deep sense of anticipation all day, her pulse and senses reeling when Jordan had arrived that evening, and she was unable to stop smiling as he and her father made polite conversation for several minutes. It hadn't even bothered her that Jordan hadn't kissed her all evening— although she deeply wanted him to kiss her now, remembering the promise in his invitation the night before.

But he seemed in no hurry even now their meal was over, pouring them both a drink, sitting opposite her in a chair rather than next to her on the sofa. He looked really wonderful in a black velvet jacket and black evening trousers, his shirt cream silk, making his hair look more golden tonight than silver.

For the first time that evening Lara felt truly tongue-tied, longing for his arms about her, and yet sensing that lack of urgency in him. Maybe he hadn't enjoyed being with her this evening as much as she had with him? Oh God, she hoped he had; she had never wanted a man's interest as much as she wanted Jordan's.

He seemed relaxed in her company; he wasn't exactly pushing her out of the door, but sipped his drink with quiet enjoyment, while the stereo played softly in the background, a compilation of romantic songs by Barbra Streisand. Maybe Jordan was waiting for some sign of encouragement from her—after all, he had been setting the mood all evening.

She put her glass down with care, nowhere near to being drunk, but very much aware of the wine she had consumed with the meal, and stood up to walk towards Jordan, very slender in a cherry-red dress in a seductive gypsy-style, her shoulders bare, the small sleeves pulled down her forearms, her only jewellery a gold choke chain. Her hair was loose and curled, secured behind one ear to flow over the other shoulder, adding to the gypsy look. Jordan's eyes had widened with apprecia-tion when he had arrived to pick her up earlier, but he had made no comment about her appearance other than that.

'Come and dance with me,' she invited huskily, taking his glass out of his hand to pull him to his feet. 'Please,' she encouraged as he made no effort to help her, resist-ing her efforts.

With a shrug he rose to his feet. 'I asked if you wanted to go out dancing after we had eaten,' he reminded her.

'And I didn't want to go—not to that kind of dancing, in front of dozens of other people. Here we can be alone, private,' she added throatily.

Jordan's mouth twisted. 'In that outfit I get the impression you should be with a tribe of other gypsies dancing around a camp-fire!'

'I'd much rather dance with you.'

'They don't have fair-haired gypsies,' he derided.

'In my camp they do.' She still held on to his hand, giving him that look beneath lowered lashes, her eyes luminous in the intimate lighting of the room.

Jordan didn't seem as immune to that seductive look as he usually was, his gaze held by hers. 'You have the strangest eyes I've ever seen,' he murmured at last.

'My gypsy eyes,' she continued to tease him. 'If you aren't careful I'll put a spell on you.'

His arms moved about her, settling her hips comfortably against his thighs as he linked his hands at the base of her spine. 'What sort of spell?'

Her arms were linked about his neck, her head thrown back as she looked straight up into his face. 'One where I have you completely in my power.'

'You don't need to put a spell on me to achieve that . . .'

Lara raised dark brows. 'I don't?' she asked throatily, enjoying this verbal flirtation.

'No. Let's dance, hmm?' he prompted softly.

It was less like dancing than swaying together in gentle harmony, caressing each other with a languor that aroused them slowly to each others needs, to a discovery of what each other liked, Lara's hands beneath Jordan's jacket as she caressed the broadness of his back.

Her head rested on his shoulder, her eyes closed as they continued to move slowly to the music. 'Why did you change your mind about me?' she murmured.

'I didn't.'

She looked up at him with a frown. 'You didn't?'

His mouth curved into a smile. 'No.'

'But you didn't like me!'

'Correction, you thought I didn't. I noticed you the minute you walked into the club with your father that day, but I usually steer clear of babies, no matter how sophisticated they are; they usually become too intense.'

'Oh.' Lara chewed on her bottom lip, her eyes downcast as she wondered if she had done exactly that.

'Which isn't to say,' he laughed softly at her woebegone expression, 'that I don't make the exception now and then.'

Somehow this didn't please her either! 'How often?'

He placed a kiss behind the lobe of the exposed ear. 'Never before, actually,' he admitted, his mouth travelling slowly round to hers.

'No?' she breathed, looking up at him, her heart in her eyes, all thought of sophistication and hiding her feelings forgotten whenever this man touched her. She had no idea what had happened to the coolly composed Lara Schofield—and she wasn't sure she wanted to! She much preferred to be the girl who was falling in love with Jordan and not afraid to show it. Or was that becoming too intense for him?

His gaze caught and held with hers. 'No.'

They both came to a halt, looking at each other for long timeless minutes before, as if by tacit agreement, they turned and walked in the direction of Jordan's bedroom.

'God, is that the time?' he exclaimed before they could reach the other room, looking down at his wristwatch.

Lara blinked up at him. 'It's only just after one.'

'And I have an early flight to Germany at six,' he

frowned. 'Would you mind very much if we postponed this?' he asked softly. 'I don't want our first time together to be rushed, with my having to hurry off to Germany in the morning.'

His thoughtfulness warmed her, and her glow returned, knowing she wouldn't want him to go in the morning if they made love now. 'Will you be away long?' she asked throatily.

'Maybe until the end of the week, I'm not really sure,' he shrugged.

'That long?' she groaned her disappointment, the empty days stretching out in front of her. 'Couldn't I just stay with you tonight, Jordan? I'm going to miss you so.' Her pride deserted her in the face of her desolation at being parted from him for the next week.

'I'll miss you too,' he touched her cheek gently, 'but I'll call you when I get back. And next time I won't send you home.'

'As you're going to do now,' she realised miserably.

'As I'm going to do now,' he nodded. 'It's better if we do wait until I get back, Lara. If I make love to you now I won't be able to think of business while I'm away—'

'But—'

'—and then I'll just have to stay in Germany longer,' he finished pointedly.

'Oh,' she grimaced her disappointment. 'But you will call me when you get back?' She looked up at him anxiously.

'I've said I will,' he dismissed tersely. 'Now I'd better get you home before your father sends out a search-party,' he derided.

'I don't think he would do that,' Lara smiled up at him as he placed her black velvet jacket about her shoulders.

'No?'

'No,' she laughed softly. 'He happens to know how I feel about you.'

Jordan's mouth was tight as he held the door open for her. 'And he doesn't mind if you spend the odd night away from home?' he rasped.

Her humour faded at the condemnation in his eyes. 'I've never stayed away from home at night.' She moved the door away from his hand, softly closing it again. 'Jordan, I don't want you to think I want to go to bed with you lightly,' she held his gaze with beseeching eyes. 'I know I'm wilful and spoilt, but I am not promiscuous.'

He bent to kiss her hard on the mouth. 'I'd better get you home,' he said harshly.

'Jordan . . . ?' Once again she felt as if she didn't really know this man at all, as if he didn't intend that she should.

'We'll talk more at the weekend, Lara,' he dismissed abruptly.

She swallowed hard, then followed him down to his car, the love she could feel growing for him making her very vulnerable where he was concerned. Maybe she shouldn't be revealing these feelings to him, but they were so new to her she had no idea how to hide them.

'I'm sorry,' she murmured softly as they drove to her home in total silence. 'I suppose babies are too intense.'

His hand came out to briefly clasp hers before returning to the steering-wheel. 'I need time to think, Lara,' he told her huskily. 'Time to know exactly where we're going. But I will call you, I promise.'

But when, that was the problem? Had she frightened him off with her eagerness, the way she had shown him how deeply attracted to him she was? She had a feeling she had.

*

Not being the most patient of people, Lara found the next week was the longest in her life, a time when she stayed in the house just willing the telephone to ring. It rang often, and more often than not was for her, but it was never Jordan.

If her father guessed the reason for her desire to stay at home he said nothing, and was unable to persuade her out of the house for any reason.

But by Friday morning Lara was becoming restless with her inactivity; she couldn't remember ever spending so much time in the house at one time before, finally calling one of her old schoolfriends and inviting her out to lunch. Her relief was immense when Melanie accepted.

'I don't think I'm suited to being a stay-at-home,' she told her father ruefully as they shared breakfast. 'I'll see you later.' She stood up to kiss him lightly on the cheek, intending to go shopping before lunch.

'Have fun.' He looked up indulgently from his newspaper. 'Leave something in the shops for all those other poor bored socialites,' he teased.

'Very funny!' she grimaced at him before leaving.

She had met Melanie Dain once a month or so since they were at finishing school together, but today Melanie's nonsensical chatter about the men she had been dating and bedding the last five weeks bored Lara. All of those men sounded as egotistical as Basil and Gary, and all she could think of was a pair of fascinating navy blue eyes, and a man who found the stupidity of social flirtations boring too.

'Are you seeing anyone?' Melanie asked with raised brows.

Lara debated whether or not to tell her friend about Jordan, and then decided against it. She wasn't at all sure of the relationship herself, the last thing she needed was to talk about it. Jordan might not even call when he got back!

It was something she didn't even want to consider. Of course he would call her!

She bought two new dresses, a pair of orange silk lounge trousers and a matching blouse, and a frivolous hat in net and lace, not even knowing when she would wear the latter. Maybe Ascot next year; there would certainly be little occasion for her to wear it before then. She was not really into hats, and had bought this one mainly out of boredom.

'I see you took me at my word and had fun,' her father grimaced as she arrived home in time to join him for tea, leaving her parcels in the bedroom for the maid to unpack.

Lara shrugged uninterestedly, the purchases already forgotten. 'I tried. Any telephone calls for me?' She tried to keep the eagerness out of her voice, although her gaze was anxious.

'Not that I know of,' her father shook his head. 'If there was no one left a message.'

She sighed deeply, pouring their tea. 'What are you doing at home this time of day?' She sat back in her chair, ignoring the cakes and sandwiches on the tray, not feeling hungry. 'Didn't you go in to work today?'

He smiled like a little boy who had played truant. 'I took the day off.'

'That isn't like you,' she mused. 'Not that I'm complaining,' she added hastily at his raised brows. 'You know I think you work too hard anyway.'

'Thank you, darling. As if happens I had lunch at the club and then played a round of golf.'

'Did you win?'

'Against Jordan?' he scorned. 'I think the last time

must have been a fluke—the man is good enough to be a champion. He—'

'Jordan?' she echoed sharply, taken aback for several seconds. 'Was Jordan Sinclair at the club today?'

'He telephoned, and I—'

'But I thought you said there hadn't been any calls for me,' she accused angrily.

'Jordan telephoned me, Lara,' her father explained gently. 'Is it Jordan you've been moping about here for?' he groaned at his stupidity. 'You haven't seen him since last week and I just assumed it was someone else who had you in this state. I'm sorry, darling, I hadn't realised.' He shook his head as he saw the tears glistening in her eyes.

'When—' she made an effort to stop her bottom lip trembling, 'when did he get back?'

'He didn't mention that he'd been away . . .' her father trailed off as she gave a pained cry, compassion for her in his face. 'Lara—!' he called after her as she stood up to rush from the room.

Jordan hadn't mentioned being away to her father, and yet the two of them had been together most of the day, by the sound of it! Was it possible that he *hadn't* been away, that it was his way of fobbing off an 'intense baby', no matter how sophisticated he had found her to be? She would have no idea if he had been seen about town this week, would she, not when she had stayed at home waiting for him.

Damn him! Her hands clenched into fists at her sides as she stared out of her bedroom window, seeing none of the city of London spread out before her. She would show Jordan Sinclair that he couldn't make a fool of Lara Schofield, *no* man did that! If he thought he was the one to end their relationship then he was wrong, there were plenty of men only too willing to help her forget Jordan Sinclair.

'Lara . . . ?' Her father raised startled brows as she walked into the lounge later that evening dressed to go out. 'I thought you were upset, that—'

'I'm going to Gary's party,' she told him brittlely. 'Don't wait up for me,' she advised with a meaningful smile.

'Lara, don't be hasty.' He stood up. 'I'm sure that if Jordan—'

'I have to go, Daddy,' she cut in brightly. Her smoky grey dress clinging to her in all the right places, one of her new acquisitions from this afternoon, a light woollen dress that revealed she wore little beneath its alluring lines. 'I don't want to miss any of the fun,' she added hardly.

'Darling, please don't—'

'See you later!' She breezed out of the room, not prepared to be persuaded by her father that she was making a mistake going out in this reckless frame of mind. She knew she was behaving recklessly, and she didn't care!

Her air of bright nonchalance lasted until she reached the waiting taxi, then anger once again took over. She had never fallen in love before, never wanted any man's love and respect as she had wanted Jordan's. But his interest in her had only lasted for two dates, then she had begun to bore him; he had even started beating her father at golf again, no longer needing parental approval now that he was no longer interested in the daughter.

The party was in full swing long before she arrived, the music loud, the conversation barely audible over its noise. But Lara wasn't interested in conversation, the wine that flowed freely tasting wonderful to her tonight, Gary Ridgeway the most attractive man she had ever met in her alcohol-fogged glow.

'Why tonight, Lara?' he groaned his frustration with the people crowded into his house, holding her intimately against him as they danced slowly to the music that could hardly be deciphered as tuneful. 'You'll stay after everyone else has left?' he urged eagerly.

Well, at least he wasn't going to attempt to seduce her in his bedroom in the middle of the party as Basil had tried to! Perhaps he had sexual finesse after all; most of her friends certainly seemed to think so. 'Why not?' she smiled up at him dreamily, her arms clinging about his throat.

He smiled his triumph. 'Why not, indeed?'

'Could I cut in?' an icy voice queried softly. 'Ridgeway?' Jordan prompted coldly as he received no response. 'You can't monopolise Lara all night.'

'Can't I?' Gary returned nastily, his arm firmly about Lara's waist as they turned to face the other man.

'Yes, why can't he?' Lara heard herself taunt defiantly, leaning against Gary so that her body rested provocatively against him.

'Who let you in anyway, Sinclair?' Gary was brave in the crowded room. 'I don't remember inviting you.'

'I let myself in,' the other man told him coldly. 'I came to get Lara.' He turned icy blue eyes on her, his gaze raking over her contemptuously, noticing everything about her, from her fevered eyes to her kiss-smudged lip-gloss. 'Your father would like you home. Now.'

She flushed at the rebuke in his tone, the shock of seeing him here fading as anger once more took over. Who did he think he was, coming here to take her home as if she were a naughty little girl who needed chastising! 'Daddy knows where I am,' she defended as haughtily as she could when her legs seemed to be having trouble supporting her.

Jordan nodded coldly. 'I think that's the reason he wants you home.'

'Why, you—'

'Get out, Sinclair,' Gary drawled insolently. 'The lady would rather stay here with me.'

'Would she?' Jordan answered the other man, but his steely gaze was fixed on Lara's flushed face. 'Lara, I'm in no mood for this,' he warned suddenly. 'I didn't expect to have to chase over half of London looking for you.'

'What did you expect?' she scorned, swaying slightly. 'That I would be sitting meekly at home waiting for you?'

'Was that too much to ask?' he rasped. 'Did you have to go out and throw yourself at the first available man who would take you to bed?' He looked at Gary with open disdain. 'Couldn't you at least have waited for my call?'

'But you did call, Jordan,' she taunted. 'My father. He said you hadn't mentioned your trip to Germany; did it go well?' Her sarcasm was obvious.

He gave a ragged sigh. 'Either you leave with me now, Lara, or you stay here with Ridgeway.' He looked at her steadily for several minutes, turning on his heel to leave as the light of challenge remained in her eyes.

Suddenly she was galvanised into action, knowing that if she let him walk away now she would never see him again. She ran after him, clutching at his arm. 'Did you really go to Germany?' Her eyes pleaded with him to say yes.

His mouth twisted as he looked down at her. 'I really went,' he nodded.

'Then why didn't you call me when you got back?'

'I did,' he answered distantly.

'When?' she blinked her puzzlement. 'Jordan, I waited all week, and I didn't get a call from you!'

'Lara, what's going on?' Gary rasped, obviously tired of being ignored when moments ago she had been all over him. 'What is it between you two, anyway?' he frowned.

'Lara?' Jordan prompted softly.

She swallowed hard, turning to Gary. 'I think I'd better go with Jordan,' she spoke huskily. 'I—I'm sorry,' she chewed on her bottom lip.

'You're a damned little tease!' he snarled. 'One of these days—!'

'That day has arrived, my friend,' Jordan told him grimly, taking a firm hold of Lara's arm. 'Believe me, it's arrived!'

He was silent in the car, and Lara eyed him nervously, not liking the angry set to his mouth at all. Finally she couldn't stand it any longer, feeling compelled to at least try and exonerate herself from the disgust she could see written in his face.

'I waited all week for you to call,' she told him again. 'A long miserable week when I didn't so much as leave the house. And then this afternoon Daddy told me the two of you had played golf together today.' Her hands moved together nervously. 'You had time to play golf with him, but not time to see me!' she accused emotionally.

He turned briefly to give her a cold look. 'You're drunk,' he stated with contempt.

'No, I—'

'You believed something had been denied you and so you hit out at the object of your anger,' he derided with sarcasm. 'You're a spoilt little girl, Lara, not a woman at all. And I think it's time you became the latter.' He stopped the car outside his apartment. 'But I don't want you drunk,' he turned to her. 'I want you stone-cold sober when I make love to you, want you to know exactly *who* it is making love to you.' He got out of the car, coming round to pull her out beside him. 'Now walk!' he ordered roughly.

'But it's raining!'

'Walk, damn you!' His eyes glittered at her until she began to stumble along beside him, the soft rain quickly wetting them both. 'And listen,' he rasped, his hands thrust into the pockets of the black trousers of his dinner suit. 'I telephoned your house this morning, and before I could ask to speak to you your father explained that you were out for the morning with an old school friend. He then asked me if I'd care for a game of golf. I arrived back from Germany late last night, I was feeling tense and in need of a break, so I accepted. When I tried to call you this evening your father told me you'd gone off to Ridgeway's party in a very reckless frame of mind. Your father was worried about you. I can see why now.' His expression was rigid with disgust.

The cold rain on her face and the brisk pace Jordan was walking were sobering her up very quickly, and she was filled with as much self-disgust as he obviously felt for her, knowing she had genuinely intended to go to bed with Gary just to spite Jordan—and knowing he knew it too! 'I'm sorry,' she said miserably, the rain dripping down her hair and over her face.

'And that makes it all right, does it?' he ground out, grasping her arms to roughly shake her, his hair a very dark blond in its wet state. 'I have to get you out of yet another potentially dangerous situation and you tell me you're sorry! God, girl, but you're stupid! Or maybe you just don't care,' he scorned. 'How many times have you slept with Ridgeway in the past?'

Lara shook her head. 'I haven't—'

'God, don't tell me he's one of the men you missed out,' Jordan derided with contempt. 'Do you have so little respect for yourself that you don't care who you go to bed with?'

'It wasn't like that, Jordan,' she choked. 'I was hurt, and I—'

'Wanted to hit out at me,' he finished hardly. 'Going to bed with another man isn't guaranteed to do that, Lara. There have been too many men in your past for one more to bother me!'

She was very pale, never having been spoken to with such disgust before. She began to shiver as the rain soaked through her dress to the skin below, knowing she must look a mess, her hair bedraggled about her face, her make-up starting to streak, the grey dress clinging limply to her body.

'Hell!' Jordan swore softly as he seemed to notice her appearance for the first time, taking off his black jacket to drape it about her shoulders, his shirt quickly sticking to his wet body.

'No, I couldn't—'

'You will,' he told her grimly, holding the lapels of the jacket firmly together in front of her. 'Sober now?' he taunted.

'Yes,' she gulped miserably, too numbed by his anger to even try and defend herself. Let him believe what he wanted, he had finished with her after tonight anyway.

'Then we'd better get inside,' he said briskly, taking her arm as they crossed the street to his apartment.

Lara simply followed him, too full of self-pity to care even when he led her to his bedroom and began to strip off her wet clothing, standing naked before him as he wrapped a black towelling robe about her body.

Jordan frowned at her lack of emotion. 'Into the shower with you.' He pushed her into the adjoining bathroom, turning the taps on until he had the water at the right temperature. 'Can you manage now?' he queried softly as she made no effort to move, huddled down in the towelling robe.

She looked at him with dull eyes, noticing for the first time how the white shirt and black trousers clung to him damply. 'Aren't you going to shower yourself; you're even wetter than I am?'

'I'll use the other bathroom,' he dismissed, frowning at her again. 'Lara, are you all right?'

'I'm fine,' she nodded.

He seemed to hesitate, then with a shrug of dismissal he left her, taking a dry shirt and trousers with him out of the wardrobe.

Lara's teeth were chattering with the cold by this time, even the warmth of the apartment doing little to alleviate the chill that seemed to go right through to her bones. The shower helped, although she still felt numb, completely sober now, filled with a shame she hadn't even considered when she had left her home so angrily earlier that evening.

Once back in the bedroom after her shower it was this shame that finally made her break down and cry, the tears falling quickly, her misery complete. She was exactly what both her father and Jordan thought of her, a spoilt brat who couldn't stand to be denied anything.

'Lara . . . ?'

She looked up to find Jordan had returned to the bedroom without her being aware of it, showered himself now, dressed in denims and a casual shirt. She quickly wiped the tears away with the back of her hand and stood up to brush her hair. 'I'll be ready in a—Oh!' She looked up at him with wide eyes as he turned her roughly to face him.

'Why are you crying?' he rasped.

'Just reaction, I think,' she dismissed lightly. 'Haven't you heard that drunks cry easily?' she added brittly.

He released her abruptly. 'Do you need any help?'

'No—thank you,' she added curtly. 'I won't be long. I just have to try and untangle my hair.'

Her hair was still damp when she joined him in the lounge ten minutes later, although she had managed to brush it partly dry. Her make-up had been irreparable, so she had cleansed it all off, knowing she must look very young as she faced Jordan across the room.

He turned from pouring two glasses of brandy, his eyes narrowing. 'Feeling better?' He held out one of the brandy glasses to her.

'Yes, thank you. I won't, thank you,' she refused the brandy.

' "Hair of the dog that bit you"?' he taunted.

She shuddered. 'No, thanks.'

Jordan's gaze was brooding as he continued to look at her. 'You're very pale.'

'No make-up,' she dismissed tautly. 'Are my clothes dry? I should be leaving now.'

'Leave?' His brows rose. 'Who said anything about your leaving?' He slowly sipped his brandy.

'My father—'

'Knows you're with me. I called him while you were taking your shower.'

'Oh.' Lara chewed on her bottom lip. 'Did he—did he say anything?'

'About your being with me?' he said thoughtfully. 'Nothing at all. He just seemed relieved that I'd found you. Have you always been this much of a worry to him?'

She bit her lip at Jordan's derisive tone. 'I don't know—probably.' She was agitated by the question. '*Are* my clothes dry?' she repeated, her eyes huge in her pale face.

'No.' His mouth was tight, the brandy seeming to

have little effect on him as he drank it down in one swallow.

'Oh.' She was becoming more worried by the second, not liking his mood at all. Surely he couldn't really have meant his threat to her at Gary's party and out in the rain just now? He couldn't want to make love to her just to *teach her a lesson*! 'Could I borrow something of yours to go home in?' she asked tentatively.

Jordan looked pointedly at the difference in their height and build, lingering on the creamy expanse of her breasts visible at the vee-neckline of the robe. 'Hardly,' he drawled.

Lara moistened her lips nervously. 'Perhaps—'

'No!' he bit out abruptly.

Her lids flew wide in surprise, panic in the grey-black depths of her eyes. 'No?' she echoed shakily.

'No.' He put his brandy glass down and walked determinedly towards her. 'You've teased one man too many, Lara,' he told her gratingly, his fingers gripping her shoulders.

She shook her head. 'But I haven't—'

'Teased me?' he finished with a dangerous glitter of his eyes. 'You've done little else since the moment we met. And you've managed to keep half a dozen other men happy at the same time,' he added bitingly. 'Well, now it's my turn. Let's make it something we'll both remember, shall we?'

Lara had never felt as vulnerable in her life before as she did at this moment. Jordan was a stranger to her in this mood—a stranger to her anyway! She might have fallen in love with him, but she knew absolutely nothing about him except what her father had managed to find out, and that hadn't really been so much. 'It's getting late—'

'Only ten-thirty,' he derided her nervousness.

'Jordan, I've never done this sort of thing before!'

'Spare me that,' he dismissed with weary contempt. 'It can so easily be disproved.'

'And it will be!' she glared at him.

For a moment, and only for a moment, he seemed to hesitate. Then the determination was back in his face as he turned her back in the direction of his bedroom.

'Jordan, please!' She had to try and convince him of the truth one more time. 'I've apologised for my impetuous behaviour earlier. Don't do this to me!' she pleaded as he remained implacable.

He closed the bedroom door behind them. The room was in darkness except for the moonlight shining through the open curtains, this penthouse apartment being on the twelfth floor. 'I promise I won't do anything to you that you don't like or want.' He was taking her black robe off even as he spoke.

'I don't want any of this!' Panic made her voice shake.

'You will,' he told her huskily, bending to kiss her throat as he slid the robe down her arms and dropped it to the floor, one of his hands resting possessively on her hip before slowly moving up to cup her breast. 'Oh yes, you will,' he promised as he gently nudged her down on to the bed, quickly removing his clothes before joining her.

'Do you love me, Jordan?' She looked up at him with wide apprehensive eyes.

'Love?' He seemed startled by the word, then he smiled, a smile without any real humour to it. 'Do all your men have to tell you they love you before you'll make love with them?' he derided. 'Is it part of the game you play?' he moved so that his thighs lay across hers, his hands holding her arms at her sides. 'If it makes you happy to hear it, then yes, I love you,' he shrugged, as if to say it wasn't important to him what he had to say in order to have her.

Lara knew it was only words, that he didn't really mean them, and her heart ached all the more because of it. This didn't mean a thing to Jordan, she was just a female body he could amuse himself with for half an hour. And the worst of it was that she knew she deserved this treatment from him, her behaviour since she had first met him had been both selfish and wilful.

'Does that please you?' He looked down at her with hard eyes.

She swallowed hard. 'No.'

'Good,' he scorned. 'Because the words don't really mean a lot on their own.'

'"Actions speak louder than words"?' she choked self-derisively.

'That's what you're about to find out!' His mouth claimed hers fiercely, and no further words were spoken between them.

Lara had never thought, never even considered that her first time with a man would be this—this almost-rape! Jordan was like a wild man, not an inch of her body escaping the knowledge of his lips and hands, her lack of response only seeming to make him all the more determined to dominate a response from her. But how could she respond when he showed her no gentleness, only a deep need to bend her to his will, to make her into what he wanted, a willing vessel for his desire.

Finally, with a look of glittering dislike at her pale emotionless face, he took her, cupping her bottom with both hands as his powerful thighs surged into her, and Lara cried out with the pain of such a brutal initiation to a man's body. After that she lay limply beneath him as he set the rhythm for his pleasure, breathing raggedly now, still holding her thighs into his as he drove into her fiercer and fiercer with each stroke of his body.

Lara had known only pain from the beginning, and was relieved when she felt him shudder and then lie still above her, his breathing slowly steadying to normal. And through it all, through his brutal penetration of her virginity, his savage taking of his own pleasure, not a word had passed either of their lips.

As Jordan moved to the bed at her side she stumbled to her feet, aching and sore from his savagery, wanting only to get away from him, to be alone in her humiliation. She almost fell into the bathroom, leaning weakly back on the door after locking it behind her. Then the tears came, deep racking sobs as she realised it hadn't been almost-rape at all, it had been a real one!

Maybe it had been her fault, maybe she did encourage men only to tease them when she said no. But she had never said no to Jordan. Until tonight! Tonight he had frightened her, shown her a brutal side of his nature that she had suspected but never thought to see. All veneer of sophistication had gone as he mastered and claimed her, only the savage remaining.

'Lara?'

She froze as he spoke on the other side of the door, knocking as she didn't answer him. She was too frightened to even speak to him again!

'Your clothes are out here if you want to get dressed,' he spoke again. 'I'll be waiting in the lounge to take you home.'

Lara heard the bedroom door close seconds later, waiting several minutes to make sure he had really left before going into the room. Her clothes lay in a neat pile on the bed, and she dressed hurriedly, heedless of the fact that whatever method Jordan had used to dry her dress, probably a heated dryer, it had shrunk the woollen garment to even more alluring proportions. Normally the ruination of such a beautiful dress would have angered her into a temper, but tonight she was so numb nothing seemed to penetrate her shocked mind and body, least of all a ruined dress.

Jordan was drinking whisky when she finally went out into the lounge, his gaze raking over her searchingly. What he saw made his mouth tighten, and his eyes become glacial. Lara shrank even more into herself.

'I'd better get you home,' he rasped, swallowing the last of his drink.

She made no reply, simply following him back down to the car, just wanting to crawl away and hide where no one could even guess at the humiliation and pain she had suffered tonight.

It was a silent drive to her home. Lara stared fixedly down at her hands, willing this misery over, wishing she had never set eyes on Jordan Sinclair.

Jordan turned to her after parking the car, sighing angrily at the way she flinched from his arm along the back of her chair. 'Lara—'

She pushed the door open next to her, intending to run to the house, but Jordan's hand on her arm stopped her, and she turned to him with haunted eyes.

His expression was grim. 'I think we have to talk—'

'I don't think so!' She wrenched away from him. 'You've never wanted to *talk* to me. And don't worry, Jordan, you have your wish,' she added scornfully. 'Tonight is something I shall remember for a very long time!' With a choked cry she got out of the car and ran to the house.

CHAPTER FIVE

LARA stared hollow-eyed and weary at the ceiling, know-ing that she should get up, that if she didn't soon go down her father would come looking for her. And after the hurried goodnight, and her missed breakfast this morn-ing, she would imagine he needed little inducement to do that! After briefly assuring him that she was safe and that Jordan had brought her home she had made her escape to her bedroom—and she had been here ever since, wide awake, her thoughts tortuous.

How shocked her father would be to know that the man he had entrusted with her safety had in fact done her more harm, both physically and mentally, than she had ever known in her life before! Physically she could feel the bruises he had inflicted, mentally she had been stripped of all the confidence that her life and body were her own; Jordan had cared little for her feelings the night before, forcing her to accept him. What had happened between them couldn't strictly be called rape, she real-ised that until last night she had been more than willing, but Jordan had chosen to take her then, when he had known she didn't want him.

'Lara?'

She froze as her father knocked on her bedroom door. 'Yes?' she answered wearily.

'Can I come in?' he questioned wryly.

'I—Of course.' She was very conscious of the bruises on her arms and throat, pulling the bedclothes up to her chin as the door opened and her father came over to stand beside the bed.

He looked surprised to see her still there. 'Lazy-bones!' he chided gently. 'It's after eleven, you know.'

'I overslept,' she invented, not having been asleep at all, the evidence of that in her shadowed grey eyes.

'So I see.' He frowned as he looked down at her, and Lara avoided his gaze. 'Are you angry with me, kitten?'

Her lids flew wide in her surprise. 'Why should I be angry with you?' She was genuinely puzzled.

'I overreacted again last night and sent Jordan after you,' he grimaced ruefully. 'I'm sure he wasn't gentle with you.'

She almost choked at the understatement of that remark, although her father couldn't possibly have real-ised the method with which Jordan had chosen not to be gentle. The other man gave the impression of being civilised, but she had learnt last night that that was only a façade. 'He—he made his opinion of my actions clear,' she avoided.

'I see,' he said dryly. 'So the two of you didn't part friends?'

'No!' Lara held back her shudder with effort.

Her father shook his head. 'I wouldn't be at all surprised if the two of you got married,' he derided with a chuckle. 'You argue enough to be husband and wife already!'

Her mouth tightened, her expression bleak. 'I wouldn't marry him if he were the last man in the world!'

'That isn't original, darling,' her father still smiled.

'You can't mean you would approve of such a husband for me!' she said with disgust.

He shrugged. 'You could do worse. Besides, I thought *you* approved?'

'Not any more,' she scowled. 'Jordan Sinclair is the most hateful man I know!'

Her father ruffled her hair affectionately. 'Jordan isn't

hateful at all, he just doesn't suffer fools gladly. And you've been behaving very impetuously lately. I'm afraid you still have a lot of growing up to do.'

If only he knew, she had grown up completely since last night, the self-confidence she had had practically since birth completely gone with the forcible taking of her body. She had been so helpless against Jordan's superior strength, had never felt so powerless, so much under the will of another person's wants and desires. It had left her with a sense of uncertainty, a lack of confidence about everything and everyone.

'Perhaps,' she agreed tightly, knowing it wasn't true.

'But you don't feel like growing up today, hmm?' her father teased.

'No.'

His smile deepened. 'You don't want to join me at the club for a game of golf?'

She didn't intend going anywhere where she might run into Jordan! 'I thought I might drive out to the Manor later today,' she heard herself say, having had no intention of going to their country estate until that moment. But why not go there? She could be alone, have time to think. Suddenly the idea seemed a good one.

Her father was frowning now. 'Nothing happened last night that I should know about, did it?'

'Nothing at all,' Lara answered flatly. 'I just thought it would be nice to see the old house again.'

He seemed satisfied with this explanation. 'Avoiding Jordan?' he teased.

She gave him a sharp look. 'Why should I want to do that?'

He shrugged. 'If the two of you have argued—again, then I suppose he'll be round later today to sort things out.'

'I doubt it,' she said dully. Although it was a possibility, she realised that. And she didn't want to be here if Jordan did come to the house.

Her father's mouth twisted derisively. 'But you intend being out just in case he does?'

He obviously thought she and Jordan had had some sort of lovers' tiff. In the circumstances it was probably better if he went on believing that. 'Exactly,' she confirmed.

'Okay, then,' he shrugged, walking to the door. 'I'll see you later, darling.'

Later, when she might at least feel able to face the world again, when everything had tilted back into perspective. If it ever did!

Heavens, she was being so emotional about this! She was far from the first woman to get more than she had bargained for after encouraging a man, especially a man like Jordan who made no secret of his thirst for physical relationships. But she had believed Jordan to have more control than he had, had never thought he would be so brutal with her!

Quite when she noticed the aggressive front of the bright red Ferrari appear in her driving mirror she wasn't sure, but it was gaining on her Porsche fast. She needed no confirmation as to who drove the powerful car, and she put her foot down on the accelerator, her own car as powerful as the Ferrari. But her driving wasn't as confident and controlled as Jordan's at great speed, and after a near miss with an oncoming car she slowed down to a more moderate speed, accepting the fact that whatever his reason Jordan was following her.

He made no effort to make her pull over to the side of the road, but followed at a leisurely pace, turning behind the Porsche into the long gravel driveway that went down to the Manor, coming to a halt behind her outside the house. Lara watched in the driving mirror as he swung out from behind the wheel, closing the door with a decisive thud to stride over to her. She gritted her teeth as he came to stand beside her car, forcing herself to turn and look at him through the open window.

If Jordan had suffered the same sleepless night and lack of appetite today that she had then it didn't show. His silver-blond hair was tousled by the breeze, the black sweater and black trousers moulded to the lean strength of his body. He looked every bit as self-assured as usual, making her wonder if she could have imagined the almost fevered glitter of hatred in his eyes last night—this man didn't look as if he could succumb to such an emotion!

'Jordan,' she greeted him abruptly, making no effort to get out of the car, her face still pale, her hair secured loosely at her nape to flow down her spine, the sombre brown clothing she wore, a cords suit and blouse, echoing her mood. 'Why did you follow me here?'

His gaze raked over her mercilessly, coming to rest almost defensively on her steady grey eyes as they stared coolly back at him. 'I still think we have to talk,' he ground out.

Her brows were raised in cool query. 'I can't think what about.'

'Last night,' he rasped fiercely. 'You haven't forgotten last night?'

Lara heard herself gasp, her breath held in her throat. How dared he follow her here and talk to her like this!

'No, I can see you haven't,' he said flatly. 'And neither have I.'

'Do I take that as a compliment or an insult?' Her eyes flashed grey-black.

He held on to his own temper with effort. 'You take it any way you want to,' he told her grimly.

'Then I'll take it as an insult!' she snapped.

He nodded. 'If that pleases you.'

'It does!'

'Your antipathy doesn't alter the fact that we have some things to discuss—'

'Such as what?' she cut in angrily. Whatever she had expected from this man, regret, an apology even, it certainly hadn't been that his anger would be directed at her! 'Last night you took a precocious child to your bed and I left it a woman, what's to discuss about that?' she scorned, at last getting out of the car, feeling at too much of a disadvantage as he looked down at her.

'The mere fact that you were what you were is a—'

'A virgin?' she mocked bitterly, her stance aggressive.

'—is a subject for discussion,' Jordan finished in a flinty voice.

'Really?' Lara's tone was bitter. 'Are you going to ask questions such as "How did a promiscuous little flirt like me come to be a virgin?" Or,' she paused thoughtfully. '"Will my father force you to marry me?" The answer to the first question is, mind your own business. And the answer to the second is, he would have to force me first!' She glared at him with dislike. 'There, I've asked *and* answered all the relevant questions, now we have nothing to talk about. Satisfied?'

'No,' he answered abruptly.

'Well, I am,' she said stubbornly. 'I don't want to listen to anything you have to say.'

'Well, you're going to!' Jordan grasped her arm roughly in his, his hand dropping away as she paled once again. 'What is it?' he frowned at her sharply indrawn breath. 'Surely I didn't frighten you that much last night?'

Colour instantly flooded her cheeks at the taunt in his voice. 'It isn't fright that makes me flinch away from you,' as she spoke she unbuttoned the sleeve of her blouse, pushing the material up her bared arm, 'I simply can't stand any pressure on *these*!'

Narrowed blue eyes were riveted on the purple-black bruises running the length of the front of her arm, Jordan's expression becoming shuttered as his jaw tightened. 'I did that?' he asked slowly.

'No,' she taunted scornfully, 'I walked into a door! That's the usual excuse a woman uses when a man has been rough with her, isn't it?'

He turned her arm over to view yet more bruises, ignoring her pointed sarcasm. 'Are there any more?' he queried gruffly.

'Several!' she snapped, pulling her arm away to rebutton the cuff. 'But they aren't for inspection!' She gave a ragged sigh. 'How did you know where to find me, Jordan?'

'Your father once mentioned to me that you had a house near here,' he shrugged. 'When you weren't at home and the maid told me you'd gone to the country I decided to drive out here. The fact that I caught up with you on the road helped,' he admitted dryly. 'What do you call this place?'

'Stapleton Manor,' she told him flatly. 'Jordan—'

'It's very impressive,' he interrupted, looking up at the three-storey grey-stone building.

Lara knew it was impressive; the house itself stood in forty acres of land, three gardeners were employed full-time to cope with the grounds, only the housekeeper remaining at the house, temporary staff being employed from the small village a mile away on the rare occasions Lara and her father stayed here.

But she made no attempt to enter the house now, walking slowly towards the empty stables as Jordan seemed disinclined to leave. The memories of the happy times she had spent here seemed all the stronger today, possibly because last night she had left her childhood behind for ever, and would never again be the light-hearted tease she had been.

Jordan followed her, leaning on the top of one of the stable doors, the stall empty. 'You ride?'

'I did.' She turned sharply.

'You outgrew it, hmm?'

Lara spun round angrily at his mocking tone. 'No, my father forbade me to ride a horse after Marion died!'

'She died—here?' He seemed shocked.

Lara nodded, not noticing the way he had paled, her pained thoughts inwards. 'In the woods over there,' she pointed to the denseness of trees half a mile away. 'Her horse bolted for some reason,' she spoke softly, almost to herself, remembering the panic she and her father had felt when Sable had galloped back into the cobbled courtyard without his rider, saddling horses themselves and going out to look for Marion. Her father had found her, her neck broken, the beautiful laughing blue eyes closed for ever. 'She was killed,' she told Jordan flatly. 'We moved back to London, and rarely come here any more. I'm surprised my father mentioned this place to you,' she frowned.

He shrugged. 'I told him about the house I still own in Yorkshire, I think he was just reciprocating. I had no idea your stepmother died here.' His eyes were narrowed as he looked about them. 'It seems a pity the estate is no longer used. You grew up here?' he put the question casually.

She nodded. 'Ever since Daddy and Marion were married.' She moved off with jerky movements, the memories crowding in on her. 'Mrs Edwards can give us tea before you drive back to London,' she told him pointedly, not waiting to see if he followed her, knowing that he would, that he had no intention of leaving just yet.

As she had known, the housekeeper was pleased to see them, and went off happily to get them some tea. Lara led the way into the lounge, it was a long room, a comfortable sitting area at one end, a cream grand piano in pride of position at the other. It was to this that Lara went, her fingers moving lightly over the keys.

Jordan strolled over to stand next to her. 'Your stepmother's?'

Her fingers landed heavily on the keys before she moved away. It had been a mistake to come here, a mistake not to make Jordan leave immediately. And he still hadn't talked about whatever he had come here for! 'Yes,' she confirmed abruptly. 'Now I really think you should leave.' She looked up at him challengingly.

'I haven't had my tea yet. And I'd like to see over the rest of the house—'

'No!'

'Yes.' He was suddenly standing very close, his breath stirring the loose tendrils of hair at her nape.

His proximity unnerved her, and she moved hurriedly away. 'I can hear Mrs Edwards bringing our tea,' she said thankfully.

'Afterwards, then,' he persisted.

Lara shot him an irritated look as the housekeeper came in with their tea-tray. 'If you're that interested,' she muttered, not wanting to cause a scene in front of Mrs Edwards, not wanting to distress the woman who had been with them since her father had brought Stapleton Manor almost nineteen years ago.

'I am,' Jordan drawled.

She thanked the other woman for the tea before she noiselessly left the room. 'Thinking of buying it?' she flashed at Jordan.

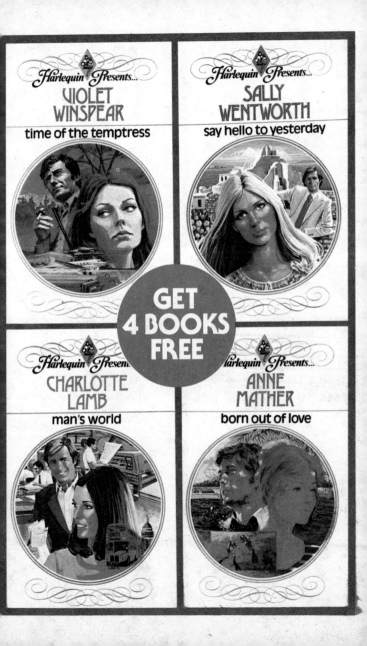

Say Hello to Yesterday
Holly Weston had done it all alone.

She had raised her small son and worked her way up to features writer for a major newspaper. Still the bitterness of the the past seven years lingered.

She had been very young when she married Nick Falconer—but old enough to lose her heart completely when he left. Despite her success in her new life, her old one haunted her.

But it was over and done with—until an assignment in Greece brought her face to face with Nick, and all she was trying to forget. . . .

Time of the Temptress
The game must be played his way!

Rebellion against a cushioned, controlled life had landed Eve Tarrant in Africa. Now only the tough mercenary Wade O'Mara stood between her and possible death in the wild, revolution-torn jungle.

But the real danger was Wade himself—he had made Eve aware of herself as a woman.

"I saved your neck, so you feel you owe me something," Wade said. "But you don't owe me a thing, Eve. Get away from me." She knew she could make him lose his head if she tried. But that wouldn't solve anything. . . .

Your Romantic Adventure Starts Here.

Born Out of Love
It had to be coincidence!

Charlotte stared at the man through a mist of confusion. It was Logan. An older Logan, of course, but unmistakably the man who had ravaged her emotions and then abandoned her all those years ago.

She ought to feel angry. She ought to feel resentful and cheated. Instead, she was apprehensive—terrified at the complications he could create.

"We are not through, Charlotte," he told her flatly. "I sometimes think we haven't even begun."

Man's World
Kate was finished with love for good.

Kate's new boss, features editor Eliot Holman, might have devastating charms—but Kate couldn't care less, even if it was obvious that he was interested in her.

Everyone, including Eliot, thought Kate was grieving over the loss of her husband, Toby. She kept it a carefully guarded secret just how cruelly Toby had treated her and how terrified she was of trusting men again.

But Eliot refused to leave her alone, which only served to infuriate her. He was no different from any other man. . .or was he?

These FOUR free Harlequin Presents novels allow you to enter the world of romance, love and desire. As a member of the Harlequin Home Subscription Plan, you can continue to experience all the moods of love. You'll be inspired by moments so real...so moving...you won't want them to end. So start your own Harlequin Presents adventure by returning the reply card below. <u>DO IT TODAY!</u>

TAKE THESE 4 BOOKS AND TOTE BAG FREE!

Mail to: Harlequin Reader Service
2504 W. Southern Avenue, Tempe, Az 85282

YES, please send me FREE and without obligation my 4 **Harlequin Presents** If you do not hear from me after I have examined my 4 FREE books, please send me the 6 new **Harlequin Presents** each month as soon as they come off the presses. I understand that I will be billed only $10.50 for all 6 books. There are no shipping and handling nor any other hidden charges. There is no minimum number of books that I have to purchase. In fact, I can cancel this arrangement at any time. The first 4 books and the tote bag are mine to keep as FREE gifts, even if I do not buy any additional books.

106 CIP BA3R

NAME	(please print)	

ADDRESS		APT. NO.

CITY	STATE	ZIP

Signature (If under 18, parent or guardian must sign).
This offer is limited to one order per household and not valid to present subscribers. We reserve the right to exercise discretion in granting membership. If price changes are necessary you will be notified. Offer expires February 28, 1985.

PRINTED IN U.S.A.

EXTRA BONUS
MAIL YOUR ORDER
TODAY AND GET A
FREE TOTE BAG
FROM HARLEQUIN.

His expression sharpened with interest. 'Is it for sale?'

Her mouth tightened. 'I would say a definite no!' She turned and walked over to where the tea-tray had been placed, and poured two cups, relieved to have something to do with her shaking hands. Couldn't Jordan see that she didn't want him here, that he was upsetting her?

She doubted he cared, he didn't give the impression that he did as he lounged in the chair opposite her, giving no indication that he even remembered forcing himself on her last night. They both sat here drinking tea like the civilised human beings Jordan had forgotten he was last night!

Her cup clattered back down on the tray, still half full. 'I'll give you the tour of the house now,' her voice was brittle. 'And then I'd like you to leave.'

He stood up to follow her with an ease that could only be called relaxed, her brief description of each room not seeming to interest him.

Lara hesitated about taking him upstairs, but the taunting twist to his mouth was enough to put the rebellious light back in her eyes, and her mouth was stubborn as she led the way to the guest bedrooms first, delaying having to reveal what had been her room since she was a child. The master bedroom was the last one she showed him before hers.

She hadn't been in her parents' room since Marion's death, the two of them often sitting together in here as Marion prepared for an evening out with Lara's father. It was a graciously beautiful room, much like the woman herself had been, the gentle lilac and cream colour scheme reflecting Marion's own beautiful nature.

'Seen enough?' Her voice was brittle.

Jordan lingered, picking up the gold and silver hairbrush that belonged to the set on the dressing-table. 'This is a lovely room.'

'Yes.' She held the door open pointedly.

'Your stepmother had good taste,' he drawled.

'Yes.' She moved out of the room.

With a last look round Jordan finally followed her, his expression remote. 'We haven't seen your room yet.'

'Shouldn't you be going now—'

'I'd like to see your room first,' he said firmly, his hand light on her arm.

Her gaze was held by his; she wanted to pull away, but was unable to. She couldn't still be attracted to him, not after what he had done to her!

'Is this it?' He pushed open the door behind her, revealing a youthfully feminine room, although there were none of the posters on the walls usually associated with a teenager; Lara always considered herself too sophisticated for that. But the bookcase contained her old childhood books that she had never been able to part with, and the quilt on the single bed was definitely youthful. 'I can see it is,' Jordan murmured as they both went into the room.

Lara felt uneasy as he closed the bedroom door behind him. 'Jordan—'

'I wasn't kind last night,' he held her gaze, his long hands framing her face. 'Maybe if I'd known you were untouched I would have been more gentle—and maybe I wouldn't,' he added ruefully. 'Do you have any idea what you were doing to me, with the string of men passing through your life?' His expression was grim.

Lara blinked her bewilderment at his sudden change of mood. Did he know what he was doing to her talking this way? Did *she* know?

'Ridgeway was the final blow as far as I was concerned,' he continued harshly. 'I'd thought of nothing but you all the time I was away, and I got back to find you out with Gary.' He scowled. 'I lost my temper with you,' he admitted. 'I think I actually hated you last night as I made love to you.'

She swallowed hard. 'I'm sure you did.' She vividly remembered the furious glitter of his eyes as his body thrust into hers, just the thought of it now making her shudder. 'Jordan, I want to go.' She tried to pull away from him, but he refused to release her.

He breathed raggedly, his eyes going black as he looked at her mouth. 'Let me love you again, Lara,' he rasped throatily. 'Let me kiss all your bruises and show you how good it can really be between us.'

'No!' Her eyes were wide with panicked fear.

'Let me, Lara,' he encouraged pleadingly. 'Let me!' His head bent and his mouth claimed hers, moving against her lips with slow drugging movements, banishing her fears as her hands curled into his shoulders instead of pounding against them to be released, her mouth opening to his like a rose in bud. Her body seemed to have a will of its own, arching against the hard strength of his in a silent pleading for the gentleness he claimed he wanted to give her.

And he did! His lips moved over every bruise he had inflicted, lingering on the creamy breasts that had known the roughness of his growth of beard last night, her blouse unbuttoned to his questing hands and lips.

She stood uncertainly before him as he undressed her fully, watching as his eyes darkened to a stormy blue. 'Jordan, I won't let you attack me like you did last night,' she told him firmly. 'I won't be used in that way.'

His answer was to claim her mouth once again, with gentleness and passion, guiding her hands to his body, encouraging her to reciprocate and take off his clothes. As she hesitated he removed his own sweater, and their bare torsoes moulded together, Jordan's chest moist and warm.

'Mrs Edwards!' Lara reminded him with a gasp.

'Knows better than to interrupt unless she's rung for,' he growled in dismissal.

She had no more objections to make, feeling a deep longing in her body for what Jordan had failed to give her last night. There had to be more to making love than Jordan had shown her in his savagery, and she had known some of the pleasure the first night he had taken her out to dinner, and felt sure he could show her much more if he wanted to.

And it seemed he wanted to, firing their lovemaking to explosive feelings as he kissed and caressed her to pulsating life. Today their bodies melted together in mutual desire, no pain, only sensation upon sensation as the hardness of his body stroked a deep need within her, a need that burst forth in a delight so wonderful she clung to him as shuddering spasms of pleasure rocked both their bodies.

'Jordan!' she sighed her satiation, still clinging to him.

'God, yes!' he breathed raggedly against her shoulder. 'Will you marry me, Lara?'

'What—?' She looked up at him with dazed eyes, sure she must be hallucinating.

'Marry me.' He leant on his elbow to look down at her. 'Will you?'

'But—' she swallowed hard, the shock of his proposal so soon after the delight of their lovemaking leaving her speechless.

'I mean it, Lara.' His expression was intent. 'Marry me.' He smoothed her damp hair away from her face where he had loosened it as they made love.

'Why?' she asked bluntly, without any real thought.

He smiled, the first time he had smiled at her in such a relaxed way. 'So that I can make love to you every night. I don't think I can live without that.'

Lara flushed her pleasure. 'It was good, wasn't it?'

He moved off her to lie at her side, his gaze never leaving her face. 'Better than last night?'

Her eyes darkened as she remembered the subjugation of last night. 'Yes.' Her voice was husky.

Jordan smoothed the frown from between her brows. 'I'm sorry for the way I was with you for your first time. I had no idea . . . You always seemed so sophisticated. I didn't realise you were just a young girl who likes to get her fingers burnt.' His eyes darkened as he looked at the numerous bruises on her creamy flesh. 'Did I kiss them all better?'

She smiled shyly. 'You know you did.'

'And I didn't inflict any more on you?'

'No'. The hot colour slowly washed over her as she remembered the gentle intimacy of his caresses.

'And your answer?'

She frowned. 'You don't have to marry me just because of—of this.'

'I know that,' he laughed. 'But *you* have to marry *me*.'

'Why?' Her voice was husky.

'I just told you, I need to be able to know I can make love to you every night.' His humour faded, his expression suddenly remote. 'Don't you love me? I thought you did.'

'Oh, I do! It's just that—' She broke off, biting her bottom lip, unable to meet and hold his probing glance.

'I did frighten you last night, didn't I,' Jordan grimaced. 'Would it make any difference if I told you that's never happened to me before? I just—I couldn't stand the thought of Ridgeway touching you,' he bit out grimly.

Lara's eyes glowed at the jealousy he admitted to, knowing that if it could always be like this with Jordan that she didn't ever want to be apart from him. Her uncertainty was reflected in the depth of her grey-black eyes.

'Marry me, Lara, and I swear I'll never touch you in that way again.'

She looked up into the navy blue eyes, seeing the sincerity of his gaze, knowing she had to believe him— because she wanted to! 'Yes, oh yes! I love you, Jordan. I love you!' They clung together until Lara felt herself drifting off to sleep, nestling into Jordan's shoulder as a beautiful drugged sleep overtook her. She knew nothing of Jordan moving across and out of the bed, pulling on his clothes with studied movements, quietly leaving the room to walk down the corridor and go into another room several doors away.

Lara stretched languorously when she woke up, feeling so different from the way she had this morning. Now she felt alive and loved, part of another human being as she never had been before. She belonged to Jordan now, intended spending the rest of her life making him happy.

But where was he? A glance at her wrist-watch told her she had been asleep over an hour. Jordan must have grown restless and gone downstairs. Lara sleepily wondered what excuse he had used to Mrs Edwards for her remaining upstairs.

The lounge and sitting-room were both deserted when she finally got downstairs, her hair brushed loosely about her shoulders, the glow in her face making up for the fact that she wore no make-up, her eyes sparkling with an inner happiness, her cheeks a nice healthy pink; she bore little resemblance to the girl with the haunted eyes who had left home this morning.

She walked outside looking for Jordan, spotting him walking across the open field that led from the woods, running over to join him, throwing herself into his arms to give him an enthusiastic kiss on the mouth.

'Do I take that to mean you still love me?' he derided, looking down at her.

She glowed up at him. 'Yes. Where have you been?' she pouted. 'I missed you.'

His arm moved across her shoulders as they continued to walk to the house. 'I went for a walk. It's beautiful countryside around here. I was wondering if your father would let us use it for our honeymoon.'

'I'm sure he would. It would bring back happy memories for him; he and Marion spent theirs here.'

'Really?' Jordan's expression hardened.

'Yes.' Lara frowned. 'Won't we be going away for our honeymoon?'

'I can't spare the time,' he shook his head. 'I'm in the middle of some rather delicate negotiations for the next few months. You don't want to wait, do you?'

'No,' she replied instantly. 'Do you?'

'No,' he echoed abruptly. 'Your father said something about your birthday being soon, next month?'

'Yes?'

'Do you have any objection to getting married then?'

Three weeks and she could be Jordan's wife! It sounded perfect. 'None at all,' she told him eagerly.

He nodded. 'The estate isn't too far from London if I have to commute in at any time.'

'Oh, you don't think you will, do you?' she groaned her disappointment.

'Let's hope not,' he said curtly. 'Although it is a possibility.'

'I refuse to even consider it,' Lara dismissed. 'We'll have a perfect honeymoon, weeks and weeks—'

'Two,' he drawled.

She gave him a pouting look, looking like a child denied some special treat.

'Two,' Jordan insisted dryly.

She sighed. 'All right, two. Two weeks of nothing to do but be together. It sounds wonderful, doesn't it?' she said dreamily.

'Is this the same girl who told me we had nothing to say to each other?' he mocked.

Lara gave a happy laugh. 'That was before I knew there could be pleasure in pain.'

He frowned darkly. 'I was gentle with you—'

'I know,' she squeezed his arm reassuringly. 'But my bruises meant it still hurt a little. It didn't matter,' she assured him as he still frowned. 'The hate wasn't there today.'

'No,' he rasped, moving away from her. 'We'd better get back to town.'

'Do we have to?' she grimaced. 'I'd much rather spend the rest of the weekend here with you.'

Jordan's expression was enigmatic as he looked around the splendour of the estate. 'It certainly is a beautiful place.'

'Perfect for bringing up children.' She eyed him mischievously.

He seemed to freeze, his mouth firming as he slowly turned to look at her. 'Children?'

'Ours,' she laughed at his astounded expression. 'You do want children, don't you?' she frowned as he gave no answering smile.

'I'm not sure,' he bit out abruptly. 'It isn't something I've ever thought about.'

Lara could have bitten her tongue for her stupidity. She and Jordan might be lovers, were going to be married, but she still knew so little about his past, his childhood. From the taut lines about his mouth she would say it hadn't been pleasant for him, that it may have affected his own desire for a family. She would have to think more carefully in future, until Jordan felt comfortable enough with her to talk about his past; not everyone had been blessed with her own happy childhood.

'It isn't important right now,' she dismissed lightly. 'We have plenty of time.'

'Yes.'

'Can we stay here tonight?' She longed to know the reassurance of his physical love for her once again.

'I think we should drive back to London. I'll come over later this evening and we can tell your father the news.'

Lara smiled. 'He'll be pleased.'

'You think so?' His mouth twisted.

'Of course.' She stood in front of him. 'Don't worry about Daddy, I can handle him.' She stood on tiptoe to kiss Jordan's firm mouth, at once feeling a stirring of the senses. 'Couldn't we just stay on for another hour or so?' she suggested throatily.

Jordan put her firmly away from him. 'It was awkward enough an hour ago when Mrs Edwards asked where you were,' he mocked.

She smiled. 'What did you tell her?'

'Nothing,' he drawled arrogantly. 'It was none of her damned business.'

'Jordan!' she giggled.

Because they had arrived separately they had to leave that way too, the Ferrari easily overtaking the Porsche, and Jordan probably arrived back at his own home long before Lara reached hers. It was only as she was locking the car door, a happy smile on her lips, that she realised Jordan hadn't once told her he loved her. But of course he did, she dismissed impatiently. Jordan just didn't find it easy to express his feelings. But he did love her, why else would he want to marry her?

CHAPTER SIX

LARA was bursting to tell her father her news when she got in, but Jordan had made her promise she wouldn't, that they should tell her father together. She knew her father would be pleased by this further formality, that since Jordan had shown such protection of her her father would have no objections to him as a son-in-law. As much as she loved her father, despite how close they were, she knew she would marry Jordan without his approval if she had to.

She and her father had been closer than a lot of daughters ever were to either of their parents, and she had never believed that anyone or anything could ever be more important to her than he was. But Jordan was. Anything he asked of her she would give him, anything at all.

The girl whose reflection glowed back at her in the full-length mirror in her bedroom had the look of love in her face, the hurt and confused girl who had left home this morning now aware of how wonderful it was to know the physical pleasure of the man she loved. She would just have to take care not to arouse the savage in Jordan again, and as it seemed to be her interest in other men that caused it she would make sure he knew he was her only interest, now and for ever.

She wore the clinging orange silk pant-suit tonight, the long sleeves and high neckline hiding the dark bruises, although they seemed to have grown in number despite Jordan's gentleness; Jordan was strong even when he was tender. But the ache in her body was a pleasurable one today, the fear of the previous night forgotten.

She could hardly contain her excitement as she waited for Jordan to arrive, glancing out of the window every few seconds as she looked for the arrival of the Ferrari.

Her father eyed her mockingly. 'Who shall I expect this evening, Basil, Nigel, or—'

'Jordan,' she told him firmly.

His brows rose. 'You've made up your argument?'

She gave a secret smile of satisfaction. 'You could say that.'

'Oh?'

'Yes, we—' she turned excitedly as the Ferrari drew to a halt outside the house. 'Jordan will explain,' she told her father as she hurried from the room to greet her fiancé.

Her heart skipped a beat as she looked at him, his silver-blond hair ruffled by the breeze, his gaze meeting hers steadily, a mocking smile to his lips as she threw herself into his arms, her mouth raised invitingly to his.

His kiss was brief. 'Later, Lara,' he drawled at her disappointed look. 'I want to talk to your father first.'

'He's waiting for us in the lounge—'

'*I* want to talk to him, Lara,' he repeated firmly, his brows raised at her rebellious pout. 'Alone,' he added pointedly.

'But why?' She still had her arms about his waist, leaning against him provocatively. 'I think Daddy is half expecting us to get married.'

Jordan's eyes narrowed. 'You told him?'

'No,' she smiled. 'I think he must have guessed how we felt about each other before we did, he said only this morning that we argue enough to already be a married couple!'

'Really?' He glanced towards the closed lounge door, his mouth thinned to a taut line. 'Then we mustn't disappoint him, must we?'

'Jordan . . . ?'

He turned back to her, the remote expression at once fading from his eyes. 'Yes?'

Lara moistened her lips at the distance he seemed to have put between them since this afternoon. 'We will be happy together, won't we? Have a happy marriage?'

His mouth tightened even more, his eyes cold. 'If you have doubts, Lara—'

'Oh no, no I don't,' she denied hastily. 'I just—No, of course I don't.' She repressed the shiver of apprehension that threatened to claim her, telling herself she was a fool. Of course she and Jordan would be happy together, all prospective bridegrooms felt tense, that was all it was. 'I'll wait in the sitting-room if you want to talk to Daddy alone.'

'I would prefer it.'

'And then later we can—can be alone?' She looked up at him hopefully, at least understanding and feeling close to Jordan in bed.

'Yes,' he answered tautly.

She claimed another kiss before going into the other room to wait for him, hearing the murmur of their voices as the two men talked quietly together. She had no doubt of her father's reaction, and knew she had been right as she received a pleased hug from him when Jordan finally allowed her to join them.

'I never thought you would have this much sense,' her father teased.

She clung to Jordan's side. 'He's a vast improvement on Nigel, don't you think?'

'Minx!' her father laughed. 'You'll have to excuse us, Jordan,' he smiled at the other man. 'I'm afraid I approved of a man for Lara that she found totally unsuitable.'

'Nigel Wentworth,' Jordan rasped in acknowledgement. 'The poor man would have been led around like a lapdog by Lara.'

She arched indignant brows. 'You think you can handle me, do you?'

He met her gaze with steady blue eyes. 'Don't you?' he mocked.

Delicate colour flooded her cheeks at the thought of how he 'handled' her, and she glanced selfconsciously at her father. He smiled at her indulgently, as if he too were aware of the intimacy that existed between the two of them.

The club the two of them went to to celebrate their engagement wasn't really what Lara had had in mind, she would have preferred a nice exclusive restaurant where they could talk instead of a noisy club where several of their mutual friends insisted they join their party for the evening. Unfortunately for Lara, Cathy Thomas was one of their number, and she didn't have the young Adonis with her tonight, and made no secret of the fact that she wished she and Jordan were still together.

'Do you have to dance so close to her?' Lara snapped when Jordan returned to the table to sit at her side after dancing with Cathy.

He shrugged, sipping his whisky. 'I'm only being sociable.'

'And she's being rather obvious!' Her eyes were stormy as she glared across the table at the other woman.

Jordan looked down at her with cold blue eyes. 'You're the one who's being obvious, Lara,' he rasped. 'And I don't like possessive woman, I never have and I never will.'

Her face became shadowed with hurt as she felt his anger. 'We're going to be married!'

His mouth twisted. 'And that means I automatically stop being aware of other women's beauty?' he derided. 'Grow up, Lara,' he bit out coldly. 'I'm as aware of Cathy's desirability now as I always have been.'

'You still—want her?' Lara was very pale.

'Yes!'

For a moment she was stunned with shock. 'Jordan . . . ?'

He gave an impatient sigh and turned towards her fully, his expression remote. 'Yes?' His irritation was barely contained.

'I thought—We're going to be married,' she repeated lamely.

'All that proves is that I desire you more than I desire Cathy!'

'Desire?' she echoed in distress. 'Is that all you feel for me?'

His mouth tightened ominously. 'This is hardly the place for this type of conversation,' he said scathingly.

'You said we would be alone tonight,' she reminded him unhappily.

'I said we would be alone *later*,' Jordan corrected harshly. 'God, Lara, don't turn into a clinging vine,' he derided cruelly. 'I won't be tied down!'

Her bewildered hurt showed in her eyes, but Jordan seemed immune to it, ordering another round of drinks for everyone before going off to dance again, although thankfully not with Cathy this time.

Lara had never been treated this way by a man before, feeling totally helpless in her love for Jordan, hating the way the women clung to him as they danced, and yet not feeling confident enough of her own power over Jordan to object too strongly again; he had already shown her how much he disliked any show of possessiveness on her part! But didn't their engagement give her the right to feel possessive about him? Obviously not, as far as Jordan was concerned. He was unlike any other man she had ever known, which was probably part of the reason she had fallen so deeply in love with him!—and she would have to tread carefully until she knew his moods better.

It was late when they finally left the club, and Jordan drove her straight home, making no effort to take her back to his apartment, much to her disappointment.

'I'm sorry,' she said miserably.

'For what?' he bit out.

'I—I don't know.'

'Then why apologise?' He didn't so much as glance at her.

'Because you seem angry with me.' She looked at him pleadingly. 'I love you so much, Jordan. I can't help being jealous of those other women.'

He made no reply, his expression harsh as he continued to drive to her home. The cul-de-sac where she lived with her father was shrouded in darkness, everything about them was quiet. Suddenly Jordan turned in his seat to pull her into his arms, his mouth fierce on hers. But Lara was becoming accustomed to his savagery, was even learning to meet it. One of his hands curved about her nape as the kiss continued, the other hand moving slowly from her throat down to cup her breast, his thumb caressing the erect tip through the silky material of her top.

His eyes glittered with repressed desire when he finally raised his head. 'Jealousy is for the young, Lara,' he rasped. 'And the fact that I talk to other women, dance with them, doesn't mean I intend going to bed with them. My relationship with Cathy was over long ago.'

'But you said—'

'That I still find her desirable,' he finished grimly. 'And I do. But Cathy wanted more from our relationship than I was prepared to give, so I had to stop seeing her.'

The other woman had given the impression that she had been the one to end the affair, and yet Lara didn't doubt Jordan for a moment when he said it had been his choice. Just as she didn't doubt that if *she* demanded more than he wanted to give he would end their relationship, even their marriage.

She moistened her lips with her tongue-tip, feeling utterly confused by the enigmatic man who was to be her husband. 'Would you like to come in—for coffee?'

His mouth twisted as he correctly read her real invitation. 'Not tonight.' He moved away from her. 'I have to leave for Germany early in the morning.'

'Again?' she groaned her dismay.

'I told you,' he shrugged, 'I have some rather delicate but urgent negotiations going on over there at the moment.'

Lara bit back her disappointment with effort. 'Will you be gone long?'

'Probably until next weekend.'

'Next—! But, Jordan—' she broke off as his face hardened into that cold mask she was coming to hate, swallowing hard at the rigid anger in his jaw. 'Friday or Saturday?' She made her tone casual, although she was secretly devastated by the fact that he was going away again.

'Friday,' he answered flatly, still displeased.

'I'll arrange a dinner party to celebrate our engagement.'

'Very well,' he nodded distantly.

'A private one,' she added throatily, looking at him beneath lowered lashes. 'For just the two of us. Here.'

Jordan's mouth twisted into a mocking smile. 'If you like,' he agreed.

She had hoped that he would like it too, but he gave no indication that he would, straightening in his seat to walk around the car and open her door for her. 'I'll call you as soon as I get back,' he told her.

Lara looked up at him with her heart in her eyes. 'And I'll make sure I'm in this time,' she attempted to lighten the tense atmosphere between them.

'Don't stay at home on my account, Lara,' he said curtly. 'Just remember that I won't be there this time if you get yourself into another awkward situation.'

She was very thoughtful as she entered the house and went up to her room. Jordan didn't act the way she expected a fiancé to act, and she knew that for once she was the one having to do all the running, that Jordan controlled everything about their relationship. And she didn't like it one bit!

Time once again dragged heavily the next week, and despite Jordan's encouragement Lara made no attempt to leave the house, hoping that he would call while he was away. When he didn't she just missed him more than ever, deeply regretted the tension that had been between them the evening they parted, wanting to do something to make up for it.

'I've been thinking,' she told her father Friday morning, 'about what I would like to give Jordan for a wedding present. If you agree, of course.' She gave him an anxious look.

Her father eyed her across the breakfast table. 'Why should you need my permission to buy Jordan a wedding present? You have enough money of your own to buy whatever you want.'

She chewed on her bottom lip. 'That's the problem, Daddy, I don't intend buying him anything, I want to give him something.' She met his gaze steadily. 'I want to give him my twenty per cent in Schofield Hotels.'

Her father frowned, then stood up slowly, walking over to the window, seeming lost in thought.

Lara stood the tension of his silence for as long as she could, finally walking over to join him. 'Daddy?' she prompted, touching his arm gently.

He turned to look down at her. 'I think we should go into my study and discuss this,' he murmured as the maid came in to clear the table.

She followed him through to the other room, frowning slightly. Somehow she hadn't expected her father to hesitate in this way. Hadn't he been the one to suggest she needed to marry a man who could take care of her business interests? She said as much to him once they were seated opposite each other across his desk.

Her father nodded. 'I did say that, yes,' he replied slowly, obviously still disturbed by what she had told him. 'And I meant it. But, darling—and please don't take this the wrong way,' he added hastily, 'this isn't meant as any personal comment against Jordan, I want you to know that. But when I said I thought you should find a man to take care of these business interests for you I meant exactly that, "take care" of them.'

'But—'

'Darling, those shares are your inheritance,' he continued firmly. 'Oh, I'll leave you rich enough when I die, but—'

'Daddy, please!' she protested with a groan.

'Just a fact of life, Lara,' he smiled, although his

humour faded almost immediately. 'But about your shares . . .'

His uncertainty worried her. 'What is it, Daddy? Why don't you like the idea?'

'How did you guess?' he grimaced. 'I'm sorry, Lara,' he ran a hand through the thickness of his hair, 'I'm not handling this very well. It's just—I'm all for Jordan controlling your business affairs; I'm sure you couldn't find anyone who could do a better job of it. But giving your shares to him . . .' he shook his head. 'I don't like it.'

'Why not?'

He sighed. 'Once you sign them over to Jordan they'll be his, and no matter what happens they will stay his.'

'No matter . . . ?' she frowned her disbelief. 'You aren't talking about divorce, Daddy? We aren't even married yet!'

'I know that, Lara, and please calm down,' he advised at the rebellious glitter in her eyes. 'I just don't see the necessity to actually give the shares to Jordan.'

'It's all I have,' she explained simply. 'All I can give him that's truly mine.'

'Exactly,' her father said with satisfaction. 'They'll make you a very rich young lady in your own right.'

'I won't need to be rich in my own right when I'm married to Jordan!'

He sighed at the logic of the statement. 'You're determined in this, aren't you?'

'Yes.'

'That's what I thought,' he nodded. 'All right, Lara, if this is what you really want I'll clear it with the other shareholders.'

'You know those old fuddy-duddys will agree with anything you say!'

'Maybe,' he smiled. 'I'm sure there'll be no problem

with Jordan taking over your shares. Especially if I make it known it's what I want.'

Her eyes lit up. 'You'll do that?'

'If it's what *you* want.'

'Oh, it is!' She threw herself into his arms. 'I want to give Jordan something that he will really value.'

'You aren't enough?' her father teased.

Lara laughed happily, her head back as she looked up at him. 'Oh, I will be, the shares will just be an added bonus.'

'Cufflinks wouldn't do, hmm?'

'No,' she smiled. 'You'll be able to convince Uncle George, Uncle David, and Uncle Sam?' she named the other shareholders in her father's business, none of them really related to her, but having grown up with them always in her life she had come to use the terms of familiarity out of respect for their senior years.

'I'm sure I will, darling,' he nodded confidently. 'Have you told Jordan about this yet?'

'I'll tell him tonight,' she said eagerly. 'I couldn't mention it before I'd talked to you. Will it all be sorted out by the wedding?' she wanted to know. 'I'd like to be able to give them to him then.'

'I'll make sure it is,' he promised.

She knew she could count on her father, and as the day passed she could hardly contain her excitement, longing to tell Jordan of her gift to him. Her father made himself absent that evening, muttering something about being in the way of young lovers.

Jordan arrived shortly before nine, and Lara could hardly contain herself until the maid had left before launching herself into his arms. 'I missed you,' she murmured between kisses. 'God, I missed you!' she groaned as his lips parted beneath the insistence of hers.

She could feel her senses swimming at his closeness,

the velvet of his blue dinner jacket feeling erotic beneath her fingertips, his shoulders strong to her touch, his cologne heady and sensual.

'Did you miss me too, darling?' She looked up at him anxiously, her heart in her eyes as she took in how handsome he was, his silver-blond hair falling rakishly across his forehead, his eyes a deep unfathomable blue. 'Please say you did.' She stood on tiptoe and kissed him once again, feeling the lack of response beneath her lips. 'Darling?' Her eyes were shadowed as she looked up at him once again.

'Of course I missed you, Lara, what sort of question is that?' he rasped, moving away from her, adjusting the cuff of his snowy white shirt. 'Did you have a good week?'

'Awful,' she told him bluntly. 'I missed you.'

'So you said,' he acknowledged tersely. 'Could I have a drink? I've had a hectic time myself.'

She hurried to pour him a glass of whisky, noticing the deep lines beside his mouth as she handed him the glass. 'You look tired.' She sat on the arm of his chair, very beautiful in a black silk dress that left her throat and arms bare, the bruises having faded completely in the last week. She caressed the hair at his nape as he swallowed half the whisky down. 'Are things still difficult in Germany?'

'Yes,' he acknowledged curtly.

'Would you—would you like to talk to me about it?'

Jordan looked up at her with mocking eyes. 'Would you understand if I did?' he taunted.

She flushed. 'No. But—'

'Then I won't bother.' He held out his empty glass to her. 'Could I have another one?'

'Of course.' She stood up, moving to the crystal decanter, eyeing him uncertainly. He was in another strange mood tonight. Perhaps once he had relaxed after his business trip he would show her some of that unrestrained desire for her she had found so overwhelming last weekend at the Manor. He was just tense at the moment that was all it was. 'Hungry?' She rejoined him, once again sitting on the arm of his chair.

'A little,' he nodded.

'Then I'll ring for dinner to be served.'

'Fine,' he accepted abruptly.

Lara didn't attempt to interrupt his deep thoughts as they ate their meal, accustomed to the same preoccupation from her father when he had a business problem. But once their meal was over she couldn't contain her excitement any longer. 'I want to talk to you about the wedding present I'm giving you,' she told him eagerly.

He frowned. 'I haven't even had time to think about mine to you. Have you made any of the wedding arrangements yet?'

She blushed. 'I've made a few enquiries. I didn't feel I should go ahead with any of them until I'd seen you again.'

'Why not?' He watched her with narrowed eyes, seated together on the sofa in the lounge.

She turned away. 'When I saw you last you were a little—I wasn't sure you wouldn't have changed your mind when you got back,' she admitted softly.

His expression darkened, and Lara felt her heart begin to race as he moved closer to her, taking her in his arms to claim her lips in a kiss that told of his deep hunger for her. She was breathless when he at last drew away, gazing up at him with starry eyes.

'Did that feel as if I'd changed my mind?' he derided.

'No,' she sighed happily.

'That's because I haven't. Now that I'm back we can begin making the arrangements in earnest. Now what have you decided to give me as a wedding gift?' he prompted indulgently, looking a little more relaxed as he settled her into the crook of his arm. 'I should warn you,' he drawled, 'I never wear pyjamas.'

'What bride would give her new husband pyjamas!' she dismissed scathingly, touching the thick swathe of hair that fell across his forehead with loving fingers. 'I've talked to Daddy, and he's sure the other shareholders will agree; I want to give you my twenty per cent in Schofield Hotels.' Her eyes glowed excitedly as she waited for his reaction.

Jordan seemed to stiffen, moving back to look down at her. 'They're your birthday gift from your father,' he frowned.

'And he's agreed I can give them to you.'

'I can't accept them,' he shook his head, his eyes cold.

'Why not?' she frowned her disappointment.

'Because they are yours, and—'

'And I want you to have them. Oh please, Jordan,' she pleaded with him. 'Let me do this.' She was surprised— and a little angry—that the two most important men in her life were proving so difficult over something she felt so strongly about.

Jordan seemed to be fighting a battle within himself. Finally he nodded, pale beneath his tan. 'All right,' he said tightly. 'If it's what you want.'

'It is,' she said fiercely.

As she had known, her father had no difficulty at all in getting his old friends to accept Jordan into their fold, and as her wedding day neared Lara couldn't have been happier about the way things were falling so neatly into place.

Only one thing marred her perfect bliss, and that was Jordan's decision that they shouldn't make love again until after they were married. It had come as a shock to her, and with her real need to feel close to him, she felt as if he were shutting her out of even a physical closeness. But he had insisted it was better this way, and with his constant trips to Germany in the weeks preceding the wedding she had to agree that perhaps it was; she wouldn't want to let him out of her sight if they were sleeping together on a permanent basis.

The wedding was everything she had ever wished for, Jordan everything she had ever dreamt of in a husband, looking very distinguished in a grey morning-suit as he waited for her to reach his side in front of the altar.

Their vows to each other were spoken softly, Jordan making his with a clear distinction that made Lara tremble with anticipation. She longed to be alone with him on their honeymoon.

The Manor had been made ready for them, Mrs Edwards taking on extra staff to help her during their stay. The lounge looked beautiful when whey arrived shortly after seven, the perfume from the vases of roses heady and exciting.

Her father had insisted that they use the master-bedroom for their stay, and it was to this room that their cases were taken. 'Would you like to change first?' Jordan offered stiffly.

She did want to change out of the yellow suit she had worn after the wedding, but she didn't want Jordan to leave her. 'Couldn't we change together?' she asked hopefully.

'Mrs Edwards is getting us a cup of tea,' he refused tersely. 'I think one of us should be downstairs to drink it.' He left the bedroom after discarding the jacket of his navy blue suit.

Lara sat down heavily on the bed. Jordan had been

very distant the last two weeks, and she had put that down to the fact that they were both under a strain because of the wedding and their decision not to make love. But the wedding and waiting were over now, and he was still holding her at a distance. Maybe he just needed time, marriage didn't seem to be something he had planned in his life for some time, if at all!

She was smiling as she stood up to undress. Poor Jordan, love had taken him completely unawares. She would just have to persuade him that it wasn't too bad once you accepted that love now controlled your life. She hadn't been expecting love herself when she met him, they would both have drastic adjustments to make to their lifestyles.

He was standing in front of one of the tall windows in the lounge when she joined him downstairs, gazing out with narrowed eyes at the field that stretched out to the dense thickness of the woods.

'Jordan?'

He turned instantly, his eyes widening at the provocation of the silver lounge suit she wore, the material moving silkily against her legs as she walked. 'I didn't pour you any tea,' he told her abruptly, walking past her to the door, carefully avoiding contact with her. 'I'll join you later. I need a shower.'

Lara didn't attempt to stop him leaving, but sat down to drink her tea, letting the tensions of the day ease out of her. She hadn't realised all the arrangements that had to be timed to happen on a certain day to make a wedding a success. And it had been a success. It had been beautiful, the sort of wedding that would be talked about for months. Of course, that sort of thing was all a bit much for a man, but Jordan had managed to conceal his impatience for the most part, although he was a little more taciturn than usual as the day progressed. A hot shower would soon relax him, then they could have dinner together. And later . . .

Later was something she was looking forward to with a wantoness that shocked her. It had been so long since she had been in his arms for anything more lingering than a brief kiss, an achingly unsatisfying kiss.

Jordan looked no less grim when he came down to join her for dinner, unsmiling, looking ruggedly handsome in a black silk shirt that was partly unbuttoned down his chest, and fitted black denims that rested low down on his hips. Lara couldn't stop looking at him, her hunger for him showing clearly in her candid grey eyes.

'Is dinner ready?' Jordan snapped. 'The buffet at the reception wouldn't have fed a bird!'

She frowned, biting her lip at his curtness. 'I'm sorry it didn't meet your approval—'

'I didn't say that,' he dismissed tersely. 'I just happen to be hungry now.'

And his hunger wasn't the same as her own, far from it! 'I'm sure Mrs Edwards is just waiting for us to say the word before serving dinner.'

'Then would you mind saying it?' His mouth twisted derisively. 'Before I expire from lack of food?'

Lara rang through for dinner, deciding that Jordan would probably be less abrupt once they had eaten; he was right, the buffet food at the wedding, as with most buffet food, was not very substantial, especially for a man.

Maybe she could have gone on believing hunger was the reason for his abruptness if he had actually seemed to enjoy the delicious meal Mrs Edwards had prepared for them, but from the little he attempted to eat she knew that wasn't the case. Something else was bothering him.

'What did Wentworth have to say?'

Lara looked over at her husband with a frown. The

two of them were drinking brandy in the lounge now, Mrs Edwards dismissed for the evening. 'Sorry?'

'Wentworth,' Jordan bit out, swirling his brandy round and round in the glass. 'The two of you were talking alone at the reception.' His head went back arrogantly. 'Was he trying to persuade you that you'd made an error in your choice of bridegroom?' he taunted.

She gave a relieved smile, at last knowing the reason for his grimness; for all that he despised the emotion, Jordan had been jealous of the few minutes she had spent talking to Nigel! 'Let's just say he was a little disappointed,' she laughed lightly.

'I'll just bet he was!' He threw some of the brandy to the back of his throat. 'I'm sure all of your friends were a little surprised at your choice of husband, the rough diamond from Yorkshire,' he added sneeringly.

Lara couldn't say she liked the way he said the word friends, almost as if it were a dirty word. But today was their wedding day, now was their wedding *night*, and she wasn't going to let anything spoil that. Jordan seemed to have a complex about his background—or lack of it— but in twenty years or so when she still loved him he would see that it was unimportant.

She stood up to move around the back of his chair, putting her arms about his neck and down over his chest, caressing the smooth hardness of his skin beneath his shirt, resting her cheek against his silver-blond hair, loving its clean lemon smell. 'You've been using my shampoo,' she teased lightly.

'It was the only one I could find,' he muttered.

She smiled into his hair, knowing he hadn't forgiven her yet for talking to Nigel. His jealousy reassured her. 'Did I tell you how beautiful I think the pendant is that you gave me as a wedding present?' She lightly touched the drop-diamond at her throat, recalling how thrilled she had been when it had been delivered before the wedding this morning, putting it on for the ceremony.

'It was the least I could do when you've given me your inheritance,' rasped Jordan; the shares were already in his possession.

Lara moved around the chair to sit between his knees, her arms linked about his neck. 'I gave you me too,' she reminded him huskily, her face lowered invitingly.

It took Jordan several seconds to accept that invitation, but his mouth finally moved towards hers, parting her lips with a groan, his arms tightening painfully about her.

Lara put all the love she had into that kiss, straining against him, her fingers becoming entwined in his hair, her mouth parted to his warm invasion, his hand cupping and holding her breast before the thumbtip began a slow caress across the hardened nub, making Lara moan her satisfaction.

'Shouldn't we go upstairs and do this?' she murmured as she kissed the strong column of his throat. 'We are married now, remember,' she teased.

Jordan looked down at her blankly, then he blinked, his expression becoming guarded. 'I haven't forgotten anything,' he bit out tautly.

She smoothed the hardness of his lean cheek with loving fingertips. 'I won't tie you down, Jordan,' she promised him intently.

'Won't you?'

She flinched at the hard disbelief in his voice. But no one had ever told her that loving a man like Jordan was going to be easy; she would just have to be patient with his cynicism about love and fidelity. 'No,' she told him lightly, standing up. 'Shall we go up to bed now?' Her voice was strained in an effort not to show him how much she wanted that.

Jordan glanced at her only briefly, moving forward to switch on the television set before sitting down again. 'You go up, I'll join you in a moment,' he told her abruptly.

She blushed at his thoughtfulness. 'I should be ready in about fifteen minutes.'

He nodded. 'Fine,' already seeming engrossed in the television programme showing.

Lara took only ten minutes in the bathroom, luxuriating in the relaxing shower-spray, before rubbing a perfumed oil over her body and putting on her white nightgown, a garment she was sure would only be worn for this one night, Jordan's virility and her own desire for him meaning she would probably sleep in the nude in future too.

The nightgown's beauty was in its simplicity, thin ribbon straps, cups of pure lace, the sheer silk clinging to the rest of her body in loving allure. The heavy weight of her hair had been brushed down her back, its dark beauty a startling contrast to the pure white silk of her gown and the honey-glow of her bare skin.

Her eyes shone with anticipation as she looked at her reflection in the full-length mirror. Soon all the tension and worry of the last few weeks would be over, all her fears evaporated by being in Jordan's arms once again, knowing the full passion of his lovemaking.

But as the minutes passed and Jordan made no effort to come to their bedroom she knew she would have to go down to him. He was still seated in front of the television when she reached the lounge, his attention intent on the screen.

'Darling?' she frowned her chagrin.

He turned to look at her, his eyes darkening to navy

blue as he took in her youthful beauty, the desire that flared in their depths like a flame.

'It's been half an hour,' she explained as he didn't answer her.

'Sorry,' he bit out. 'I got caught up in the programme. I'll just switch everything off down here and then I'll join you.'

Lara gave him a tremulous smile, forgiving him instantly. 'I'll see you in a few minutes, then.'

'Yes,' he nodded abruptly.

The 'few minutes' once again stretched into half an hour, and in her agitation Lara moved swiftly back down the stairs. Jordan still sat in the armchair staring at the television, an old black and white film showing now.

With a choked cry Lara turned on her heel and ran back up to the bedroom. She couldn't even hold Jordan's attention on their wedding night over a B-rated film!

CHAPTER SEVEN

LARA carefully arranged the roses in a vase, not seeing their dewy-soft beauty as the beautiful blooms began to take shape in a colourful array in the vase she had placed on the kitchen worktop, the cook and housekeeper they had employed on their return to London a week ago moving quietly about the kitchen behind her preparing the dinner.

'They're beautiful flowers,' Mrs Knight remarked warmly.

'Yes.' Lara put the last rose in place.

'Mr Sinclair must have bought the florist's shop,' the cook teased.

A shutter came down over Lara's eyes, leaving her cold and withdrawn. 'These didn't come from Mr Sinclair,' she said curtly. 'My father sent them as a thank-you for coming to dinner here last night.'

The other woman looked slightly uncomfortable. 'Well, they certainly are lovely, no matter who sent them.'

Lara walked through to the lounge with them, placing the vase on the dining-room table, the three dozen lemon and white roses instantly adding warmth to the lounge she still found as impersonal as when she had first seen it two months ago, becoming the most prominent feature in the colourless room. Not that she thought Jordan would notice them; he noticed very little about their married life, least of all their home.

She forced herself not to give in to the tears as she thought of their honeymoon, knowing she had done enough crying while they were at the Manor, and determined now that they were back in London that no one should know of the disaster her marriage had become. She knew that she was succeeding, that perhaps only Mrs Knight realised she and Jordan were not the happily married couple they appeared to be to other people. Even her father had been here to dinner the previous evening and not guessed the sham her marriage to Jordan had turned out to be.

Who would believe her if she told them she and Jordan had spent the whole two weeks of their honeymoon as physical strangers? She could hardly believe it herself!

Their wedding night had set the pattern for the rest of their honeymoon, Lara going to bed first, Jordan lingering downstairs watching television or listening to the stereo until he thought she was asleep. And some of those nights he slid into bed beside her she was far from asleep, had still lain awake long after she knew by the even tenor of Jordan's breathing that he was indeed sleeping. She had learnt well not to show she was awake when he came to bed; she had been sitting up in bed reading a book one evening after he came to bed two hours after her. Jordan had coldly excused himself and gone downstairs to sleep on the sofa that night, and the next morning he had returned to London for two days, on business.

Their honeymoon had been a disaster, and their return to London was no different; here they even had separate bedrooms! Lara had had no idea what had gone wrong between them, she only knew her marriage was over before it even began. And she didn't know why; she continued to stay at Jordan's apartment as his wife only because he hadn't actually asked her to leave. Her tentative questioning about what was wrong between them had been met with such coldness that after the first few attempts she had stopped asking. Jordan no longer wanted her, and there was nothing she could do now except wait for him to tell her their marriage was over.

The irony of it was that she loved him more than ever, had matured overnight, it seemed, had grown up so completely these last three weeks that the spoilt and wilful Lara Schofield no longer existed in the shell of Lara Sinclair. And still Jordan didn't want her, had shunned so many attempts by her for a closeness between them that now she didn't even try.

She turned as the doorbell rang. 'I'll get it, Mrs Knight,' she told the housekeeper and cook as she came out of the kitchen, Lara cool and beautiful in a silk dress of ice-green. 'Daddy!' she greeted him enthusiastically, putting her hand through the crook of his arm as she led him into the lounge. 'Thank you for the flowers,' she smiled up at him, her despondency of a few minutes ago completely gone as she relaxed with her father, conscious that her shield of cool confidence would have to be firmly back in place once Jordan returned home. It was the only way she could get through spending time with him; she was too proud to let him see her inner misery.

'My pleasure, darling,' he hugged her affectionately before sitting opposite her in one of the armchairs. 'All alone?' he enquired lightly.

'Except Mrs Knight,' she nodded, her hands folded demurely in her lap, bare of all adornment except the plain gold wedding band. 'Jordan is at work,' she added as her father seemed to expect something more.

He frowned. 'Yes, I know. No shopping today?' he teased her about the habitual shopping sprees she would go on when she lived at home.

'I'm a married woman now, Daddy,' her smile didn't

quite reach her eyes, 'I don't have time for frivolous afternoons at the shops.'

'Surely Mrs Knight takes care of the apartment?'

A frown appeared again between her shadowed grey eyes. 'Is all this leading up to something, Daddy?' she asked slowly.

He relaxed back in the armchair, unbuttoning the single button on his jacket, the matching navy blue waistcoat fitting tautly to his still trim body. 'I noticed last night that you were looking a little pale,' his eyes narrowed as her expression suddenly became evasive. 'Everything is all right, isn't it, darling? Between you and Jordan, I mean.'

She gave a lightly dismissive laugh, pleased when it seemed to come out so naturally. 'What could possibly be wrong, we've only been married three weeks?' and two days, and forty-six minutes. She knew, because that was the exact time this hell began for her.

'Sometimes the beginning of a marriage is when you have the trouble.'

'Not Jordan and I, Daddy,' she shook her head at his persistence. 'Can I order some tea?'

'Not for me, thanks.' He wasn't put off by her sudden change of subject. 'Is something troubling Jordan, then?'

Lara's already frayed nerves were beginning to stretch to breaking point. 'Not that I know of,' she answered tautly.

'Then why did he oppose every proposal I made at the shareholders' meeting today?'

Her eyes widened at her father's quietly voiced question, and she looked at him with strain in her face. 'He did?' she frowned. The two men had discussed today's meeting over dinner yesterday evening, and they had seemed in agreement then.

'Yes,' her father confirmed curtly. 'He's blocked the plans I made to buy more overseas, and he's delayed the selling of my hotels here,' he told her grimly.

'Can he do that?' she gasped.

'With David's help he can,' her father sighed. 'And David has always been against selling any of our holdings, and he doesn't believe the financial climate right to buy either. George and Sam chose to abstain, so we're in stalemate until the next meeting. It isn't that I mind so much—although God knows it's annoying enough—it's the fact that Jordan made no mention of his objection last night.' He gave a rueful smile. 'I didn't know if the two of you had argued and he was feeling angry with me too.' The suggestion was put lightly enough, but there was an underlying seriousness to his tone.

'Jordan doesn't do business like that,' Lara shook her head firmly.

'Do I take that to mean you have or haven't argued?' he teased.

The politely stiff conversation she and Jordan shared could in no way be thought of as arguments, especially as they never discussed anything of a personal nature. The several attempts she had made to find out what had made her husband a stranger had resulted in Jordan getting up and leaving the room. That seemed to be his answer to everything at the moment—and because she didn't want to lose him altogether she didn't press the matter.

'We haven't,' she answered truthfully.

'Then what the hell is the matter with him?' her father scowled. 'When I tried to talk to him after the meeting he said he didn't have time, that he was too busy!'

Lara's thoughts were racing now, wondering at Jordan's decision to oppose her father. She had meant it when she told her father Jordan wouldn't do it just to be spiteful to her; in business he was completely clear-headed. Perhaps he really did think the move into more overseas hotels was wrong, and that selling now wasn't a good idea. She just didn't understand, as her father didn't, why he hadn't mentioned it last night when the subject had been talked about between them at great length.

'He does have a business of his own to run, Daddy,' she soothed. 'The shares in Schofield are only secondary to him.'

'I know that. I—' he broke off, giving a weary sigh. 'I shouldn't be worrying you with this, it *is* business, not the sort of thing we should be discussing over tea.'

'You refused tea,' she reminded him with a smile.

'I've changed my mind,' he returned the smile with a rueful one of his own. 'It's thirsty work overreacting,' he added dryly. 'I'm sure this will all be sorted out at the next meeting in two weeks' time. You aren't to think about it again, kitten.'

Lara accepted his light dismissal of the subject, sensing that he regretted even mentioning it to her now, although she knew she *would* think of it.

By the time her father left an hour later he seemed to have forgotten the matter himself—seemed to have done, although she felt sure he hadn't really. Schofield Hotels had been her father's life for a long time, even more so during the years since Marion died, and he wouldn't take kindly to suddenly having the control of his company taken out of his hands. Now she was beginning to understand the problems she might have created by giving her shares to Jordan.

She knew it was no use expecting Jordan home earlier than six-thirty, and with the interruption of the shareholders' meeting into his already busy schedule he was likely to be even later than that.

The look on his face when he did come home was enough to freeze any questions she might have wanted to ask in her throat. He came into the flat like a tornado, going straight to his bedroom, having already taken off his jacket, and was in the process of removing his shirt too, his chest muscled and tanned, by the time she had followed him into the room.

After weeks of no intimacy between them Lara couldn't take her eyes off him; her breathing was suddenly shallow, the blood pulsing through her veins, soft colour flooding her cheeks. She swallowed convulsively as Jordan looked up and caught her longing expression, his mouth twisting with derision, his eyes cold.

'There's no hurry,' she told him to cover her awkwardness, her voice thin and quavery. 'Dinner won't be ready for half an hour yet.'

Jordan threw his shirt down on to the bed, the muscles in his back and chest rippling with power as he flung open the wardrobe to take out his clean clothes. 'I'm not eating here tonight,' he told her in a preoccupied voice, taking out a brown silk shirt, brown trousers and a cream dinner jacket. 'Do you know where my brown velvet bow-tie is?' He turned to her with a frown.

'Here.' She moved forward to take it out of it's usual place in his wardrobe, looking up at him with puzzled eyes. 'You're going out?'

He gave her an impatient look. 'Well, if I'm not eating here that would be the natural assumption to make,' he bit out sarcastically.

She forced herself to remain unmoved in the face of his sneering manner, having learnt to hide a lot of her emotions since she had married him. 'A business dinner?'

'Yes.' He went into the bathroom, opening the cabinet to take out his shaving things.

Perhaps it was the way he smiled to himself as he said that, or perhaps it was the way he seemed to give her a pitying look. Whatever the reason, Lara knew Jordan didn't have a business dinner this evening. For a brief moment she toyed with the idea of leaving the subject, of not wanting to know the truth, not if she was going to be hurt any more. But then her spine stiffened stubbornly, some of the old rebellious Lara surfacing to save her pride.

'Who is she, Jordan?' she asked dryly.

For a moment his eyes froze into angry black pools as he looked at her in the mirror, then he continued to shave, the movements of his hands with the razor sure and smooth. 'She?' he enquired lightly. 'Did I say I was dining with a she?'

Lara drew in a controlling breath. 'You didn't have to. So, who is she?'

He shrugged. 'No one you know.'

She swallowed hard at his calm admission of meeting another woman, feeling as if someone had just kicked her in the stomach. 'She isn't business, is she?' she choked.

Jordan strode back into the bedroom, his shave completed, stripping off the rest of his clothes with little concern for his nakedness.

'Jordan?' Lara prompted tautly, wishing she could remain unaffected by the male beauty of him. But oh, how she still ached for him!

His gaze raked over her coldly, missing nothing of the dark beauty of her hair, the light grey dress that moulded seductively to her body, her breasts pert and inviting beneath the soft material, her hips gently curved. His expression turned to one of boredom before he pulled on his black robe. 'Why don't you go out yourself, Lara?' he suggested curtly. 'I'm sure some of your old friends would like to see you again.'

They hadn't been out together at all since their marriage, and this was the first time Jordan had gone out for any reason in the evening either. 'Will it make it easier for you to have an affair if you think I'm having one too?' she bit out coldly.

He gave her a pitying glance. 'If I want to have an affair, Lara, then I'll have one,' he derided. 'I don't need your permission, either verbally or morally. Have you forgotten your promise on our honeymoon not to tie me down?' he drawled.

Three weeks of suppressing her emotions made her temper rise out of all control. 'Honeymoon?' she repeated scornfully. 'You call that—that fiasco a honeymoon?'

His brows rose in cool arrogance. 'If you aren't satisfied with our marriage, Lara, then you know where the door is.'

Her anger faded as quickly as it had begun, grey eyes reflecting her inner pain. 'Jordan, you know I didn't mean it that way,' her voice lowered pleadingly. 'I just—What went wrong?' she groaned her confusion.

'I wasn't aware that anything had,' he replied calmly, his hands thrust deep into the pockets of his robe. 'You wanted me, Lara, you wanted to be my wife. What's wrong?' he taunted coldly. 'Isn't it the "fun" you thought it would be?'

'Jordan, please—'

'I have to finish getting ready,' he dismissed abruptly. 'I don't want to be late.'

'For your mistress,' she muttered bitchily.

'She isn't yet,' he gave the facsimile of a smile, his eyes still cold blue chips. 'But I'm hoping she will be.'

'What woman could resist you?' Lara choked.

'A few have,' he answered thoughtfully. 'Although

that was never even a possibility with you, was it?' he taunted cruelly.

Lara paled, her eyes suddenly huge and dark. 'You bastard!' she said with quiet intensity.

His mouth twisted. 'So Lara Schofield lives on,' he mocked. 'I wondered.'

'Well, you won't need to wonder any more,' she told him with controlled anger. 'I'm alive and well and living in the guise of Lara Sinclair.'

'Poor little Lara,' he drawled softly, coming purposefully towards her. 'Have you missed my kisses, darling?' One long sensitive hand came up to caress the smoothness of her cheek. 'My touch?' he prompted huskily, his thumbtip gently parting her lips to probe the erotic flesh within.

'Jordan!' Was that aching groan really made by her? She knew it was as she unconsciously swayed towards him, her hands moving up to tentatively touch the firm flesh of his chest. 'Oh, Jordan . . .' Her eyes were liquid with longing as she looked up at him.

For a moment he looked down at her wordlessly, then he smiled, his hand dropping back to his side. 'Sorry, Lara, I don't have the time right now,' he mocked silkily. 'Perhaps later.'

Humiliated colour flooded her cheeks. 'You—you cruel bastard!' she burst out angrily. 'I could quite easily get a divorce for the cruelty you've shown me since the beginning of our marriage. An annulment!' she added challengingly.

'Then why don't you?' he returned calmly.

Her eyes widened with disbelief. 'I—Is that what you want?'

'It doesn't seem to be what I want that matters,' he shrugged. 'I'm sure you will do exactly as *you* please— you always have, I'm sure you always will.'

Lara swallowed hard, wishing she could bring back at least a measure of the closeness they had found that day when Jordan had followed her to the Manor. But hadn't it been a physical closeness, hadn't she sensed that even then, when Jordan hadn't told her he loved her after asking her to marry him? He had *never* told her he loved her, and he no longer wanted her physically either. 'Jordan, why did you marry me?' she asked wearily.

'Tired with being my wife already?' he taunted coldly.

Tired of *not* being his wife! What was wrong with him? What was wrong with *her* that he could no longer desire her physically? How had she changed since the afternoon he had told her that he didn't think he could live without making love to her every night?

Jordan saw the confused dismay in her face, his mouth twisting sardonically as he misread the reason for the emotion. 'So I can expect to arrive home one evening and find my little wife has run home to Daddy?'

'That night could be right now, if you really do intend going out with a mistress!'

His brows rose, his lips curved into an unpleasant smile as he walked back to the bathroom. 'I intend going out with whom I want, when I want. You must do the same.'

'Take a lover of my own?' Her voice sounded shrill now.

He shrugged. 'If it's what you want.'

'You know it isn't,' she cried. 'Jordan, you were my first and only lover. You *know* I'm not promiscuous!'

He gave an impatient sigh. 'Then I don't see the point of this conversation. I have to go, Lara. Shala doesn't like to be kept waiting.' He closed the bathroom door behind him, effectively shutting her out.

So she even knew who her rival was—Shala Newman; there couldn't be two women in London with such an unusual first name. Shala Newman was the toast of the theatre this year, a new young talent that had taken the town by storm.

But knowing who Jordan was seeing changed nothing; she wouldn't be leaving him, and there could be no annulment. She was already six weeks pregnant with Jordan's child . . .

'He's done it again!' her father exclaimed explosively two weeks later as soon as Mrs Knight had left the lounge after showing him in.

Lara put down the book she had been reading, finding no difficulty in doing so; she had little concentration for anything these days. She hadn't seen her father for almost a week, since he had telephoned and persuaded her to go out to lunch with him one day. It had been a welcome break from the apartment, with Jordan out at work all day, out most evenings too now. His relationship with Shala Newman had obviously progressed as he wanted it to.

She felt sure her father, a very social man, had heard the rumours of Jordan's affairs, but he hadn't mentioned it last week and he didn't seem in the mood to discuss it now either.

'Sit down, Daddy.' She stood up. 'You'll give yourself a coronary rushing around like this!'

'I wouldn't need to "rush around" if that husband of yours weren't so unpredictable,' he scowled, but sat down anyway. 'I spoke to him on the telephone only this morning, and he said he was giving a lot of thought to the proposals I made at the last meeting.'

Lara gave a deep sigh, sitting back on the sofa. 'And what did he decide after he had thought?'

'To oppose me, of course,' her father frowned. 'I don't know what's the matter with the man!'

'Because he doesn't agree with you?' she teased light-ly, knowing there had to be more to it than that. 'That doesn't mean there's anything wrong with him, Daddy. I thought you liked the fact that he's an independent man, that he won't be pushed around. By anyone,' she added tautly.

'That doesn't mean he can ruin me—Oh, it isn't that serious,' he amended lightly as he saw the way she paled.

'Daddy?' she prompted, knowing he was making light of this. 'Jordan's opposition could really ruin you?'

'No—'

'The truth,' she demanded tautly. 'I'm no longer a child you have to shield from life,' she reminded him softly, knowing she would never be a child again.

'No, you aren't, are you?' Her father looked at her closely for the first time since he had arrived. 'You don't look well, darling,' he frowned his concern for the dark circles beneath luminous grey eyes, the nervous move-ments of her hands.

'I'm fine,' she gave a deceptively bright smile. 'I've had a slight cold, that's all.'

He didn't look convinced. 'You look as if you could do with a holiday. When are you and Jordan going to have a proper honeymoon?'

She turned away. 'Jordan doesn't have the time right now, he's very busy.'

'I know that,' he nodded grimly.

'So tell me,' she sighed. 'Can he really hurt you with his opposition?' She held her father's gaze steadily, refusing to let him break the contact.

Dull red colour crept up his lean cheeks. 'Over these few issues, no,' he finally answered quietly. 'But if he keeps it up at every meeting then, yes, he can hurt me,' he admitted heavily. 'More than I care to think about.'

Lara moistened her lips with the tip of her tongue. 'And does he realise that?'

'If he doesn't he isn't the businessman I thought he was!' her father scowled. 'Yes, I would say he knows exactly what he's doing. What I don't understand is why!'

Neither did she; all she did know was that Jordan was deliberately punishing her father and herself for some reason. He had to know his coldness was hurting her, and he *was* too good a businessman not to know exactly what his blocking actions were doing to her father. If only she knew *why*, if only he would talk to her!

But she could count the occasions she had seen her husband alone the last two weeks on one hand, his evenings—and sometimes his nights too, by the look of his unslept-in bed in the mornings, completely taken up with Shala Newman. Several times she had been tempted to take his advice and go out herself, knowing that it was what the old Lara would have done without a second thought. But she was carrying Jordan's child inside her, was determined that child would know him as its father. Her pride wouldn't let her tell Jordan of the child, she just hoped that when her pregnancy became noticeable Jordan would once again notice her too!

'Have you asked him?' she frowned now.

Her father nodded. 'He refused to discuss it.'

'Maybe he has his reasons, Daddy—'

'Then why refuse to talk to me about them?' he scowled. 'I just don't understand the man, Lara.'

Neither did she, but she had a feeling, for her father's sake, that it was time she did. She had never understood the man she had married, the man she loved, had only known that she wanted to belong to him. But now it was time they talked, time she knew what demon was driving him on to her father's destruction as well as her own.

Jordan was late home that evening, his expression not encouraging when she chanced a glance at him. But she resolutely followed him anyway, receiving a cold look as he turned to see her in his bedroom.

'I want to talk to you,' she told him softly.

'Again?' he derided mockingly. 'I wonder why you always feel this burning need to talk to me after a Schofield shareholders' meeting?'

She flushed at the taunt. 'My father is worried—'

'He's been here?' Jordan's eyes were flinty.

Lara sighed. 'Yes. He—'

'Came running to his daughter for advice on how to handle her husband?' he rasped. 'I hope you told him you have no idea,' he scorned, taking his black dinner suit out of the wardrobe.

Lara felt her heart sink as she looked at the suit. 'You're going out again?'

His dark blue gaze moved over her contemptuously. 'And what if I am?'

'With Shala Newman?'

His mouth twisted. 'As a matter of fact, no. I find my—interest no more lasting than it used to be,' he drawled.

Lara flinched at the taunt; his interest in her was certainly not enduring. 'Who it is now, Jordan?' she tortured herself.

'You remember Cathy?' he mocked softly.

'Cathy Thomas?' Her lips felt stiff.

'Mm,' he nodded.

'You—you're seeing her again?' Lara gasped.

'I told you I still found her attractive,' he shrugged.

Lara sat down in the bedroom chair, suddenly feeling weak. 'Jordan, why are you doing this?' She stared down sightlessly at the carpet. 'Why are you trying to hurt me?' Tears shimmered in her eyes as she finally felt brave enough to look at him once again. 'Why are you hurting my father?'

'I haven't so much as touched your father,' he rasped, suddenly tense.

'You know what I mean. You're using his own business to try and hurt him. I didn't give you those shares so that you could do that to him!'

'But you did give them to me,' he reminded her with menace. 'And now I have the right to make what decisions I see fit.'

'But eventually that could ruin my father!'

'Yes,' he bit out, his face twisted savagely.

Lara's eyes widened at the ferocious glitter in his eyes, the white ring of tension about his mouth. 'That's what you want, isn't it?' she realised incredulously. 'What you've wanted to do all along?' Suddenly it was all becoming clear to her.

'Yes,' he acknowledged with fierce pleasure.

'But why?' she groaned. 'What did Daddy ever do to you? What did *I* ever do,' she added bewilderedly, 'to make you hate me?'

'I don't hate *you*, Lara,' he denied impatiently. 'You just got in my way.'

'My father, then?'

'Yes!' he bit out harshly. 'I hate him. I hate what he took from me, what you both took from me!'

Lara swallowed hard, seeing Jordan as a man in torment, a man racked with revenge, a need to make her father and her suffer. But she still didn't know *why*! 'We didn't even know you until a few months ago, how can you hate Daddy when *he* didn't even know of your existence?'

Jordan was breathing hard, his teeth bared savagely. 'It's for that very reason I hate him,' he rasped. 'He *did* know of my existence, and yet he still didn't give a damn.

He took what he wanted and to hell with the rest of us!'

She still didn't understand him, rubbing her temple with trembling fingertips as it began to throb with a piercing pain. 'I don't understand,' she said dully. 'Did Daddy force you out of a business deal?' she frowned. 'If he did I'm sure he didn't realise it. I've never known my father to be anything other than completely fair.'

'Haven't you?' Jordan scorned derisively. 'Then perhaps you don't know your father as well as you thought you did. But he's hurting now, and he'll hurt even more in the future,' he stated coldly. 'The way I was hurt all those years ago. You still haven't realised, have you, Lara?' he taunted softly. 'Still don't know what all this is about?'

She shook her head. 'No.'

'No,' he gave a hard, humourless laugh. 'Look at me, Lara, look at me closely. And tell me if you can see any resemblance. My father always told me I looked most like my mother.'

A deep frown grooved between her eyes. 'Your— mother?'

'Yes,' he grated, his eyes narrowed to steely slits. 'My mother. Marion,' he bit out as she still looked puzzled. 'I'm Marion's son, the son she had before she met your father and he persuaded her to become his mistress!'

CHAPTER EIGHT

LARA stared at him with uncomprehending horror. She didn't know what he was talking about. Marion had been a widow when Lara's father met her, a *childless* widow. Jordan had made some ghastly mistake, had made them all suffer for nothing.

She shook her head. 'Marion didn't have a son—'

'Look at me, Lara,' he repeated tautly. 'Look at me and then try telling me that again.'

She blinked, doing as he instructed, her face becoming even paler as she did so. Jordan's hair was more silver than golden, his eyes navy instead of pansy blue, his features hard and unyielding instead of serenely beautiful. And yet she could see the resemblance he claimed, the shape of his face, the wide forehead and sensitive eyes.

'Maybe this will convince you.' He took his wallet from his breast pocket, pulling out an old and worn photograph, as if it had been handled many times. He thrust it at her.

Lara's hand shook as she accepted the photograph, and she gave a small gasp of dismay as she recognised the woman in the wedding photograph. It might have been taken over thirty years ago, but Marion was still recognisable as the bride, the man standing at her side having Jordan's other dominant features, the firm mouth and thrusting chin, the tall and muscular body. The man was definitely Jordan's father, and with Marion as his bride it would seem obvious that she was Jordan's mother.

Lara swallowed hard, staring wordlessly at the photo-

146

graph. God, no wonder her father had begun to have Marion so prominently on his mind shortly after meeting Jordan! This man was the son of the woman he loved!

She looked up at Jordan with pained eyes. 'We never knew,' she shook her head compassionately.

He took back the photograph, putting it back in his wallet, taking care not to crush it. 'You may not have done,' he spat out, his eyes blazing, 'but your father certainly did!'

'No—'

'Yes!' he hissed. 'I even met him once, briefly. Although my mother was very careful that that didn't happen again,' he derided hardly. 'Too afraid I might mention it to my father, I suppose. And your father certainly didn't want to get involved with me, he didn't want some other man's child dragging along. All he wanted was my mother,' he rasped. 'And he took her away from my father and me to get her!'

'I can't believe that!' Lara gasped.

'Why can't you?' he scorned. 'My mother came to live with you, didn't she? Became *your* mother. You didn't notice a ten-year-old son with her, did you?'

She could have cried for the bitterness that drove him, although she knew he had to be wrong. Her father would never have been so cruel as to push Marion's son from her life, and Marion would never have left her child, she was too loving a woman for that.

'I can't believe she abandoned you—'

'She left me with my father!' Jordan told her tautly.

'Well, that often happens in a divorce—'

'There was no divorce.'

Lara stared at him with wide eyes. 'No—no divorce?' she asked dazedly.

'No,' he scorned. 'I told you my mother left to become

your father's mistress, and that's what she stayed. She was never married to him.'

This was too much to take in, and she knew it couldn't be the truth either. For fifteen years her father and Marion had celebrated their wedding anniversary in March, that couldn't have all been a lie. Could it? Jordan seemed convinced that it was. But he had to be wrong! She might have been too young to remember the wedding, but her father and Marion had always acted like husband and wife. Acted? She was beginning to sound suspicious herself now!

'My father refused to divorce her,' Jordan continued bitterly. 'He probably kept hoping that she would eventually come back to him.'

'Probably hoped?' she echoed. God, she sounded like a parrot! she thought hysterically.

Jordan's fierce gaze cut into her. 'He died when I was fourteen,' he rasped. 'I was adopted by his sister and her husband, which is how I finally learnt the truth about my mother. I thought she was dead, you see,' he revealed scornfully. 'My aunt took great pleasure in telling me the truth.'

Lara swallowed hard, knowing now that she had only ever been a pawn in a rather cruel revenge, that her marriage had only existed for her, never for Jordan.

'My father and I were living in Hong Kong when he died, my aunt and uncle flew out and brought me back to England. They even adopted me as their own and changed my name to theirs,' he added harshly. 'Not that I minded that, it's given me the shield I needed to seek out the man who seduced my mother away from her own husband and child.'

'Marion and my father loved each other!'

'Perhaps they did,' his eyes glittered with a chilling coldness, 'but that still doesn't excuse the selfishness of their love. I never saw my mother again after the day she walked out on us, and my father found his pain easier to bear by believing she was dead. My aunt knew better,' Jordan bit out coldly. 'She even knew the name of the man my mother left with. He was easily traceable,' he added mockingly.

'But why wait until now for your revenge?' Lara cried her bewilderment. 'Marion only died five years ago. You could have met her, spoken to her, let her tell you the way things really happened—'

'I know how they happened!' he snapped with barely controlled vehemence. 'The pain of my mother leaving us almost killed my father! We left England, his memories, to travel around the world, looking for God knows what!' He was finally revealing the bitterness of the first fourteen years of his life, and it was so much worse than Lara had ever imagined. 'We never stayed in one place for long, we were always moving on. My father began to drink, heavily, and it finally killed him.'

'Oh no!' Lara gasped her horror.

'Oh yes,' he nodded grimly, his mouth tight. 'The night my aunt told me about Joseph Schofield I decided I would make him pay for what he had done. But I couldn't do it as a penniless youth, I had to have the means at my disposal to make it a suitable revenge, be a powerful adversary for your father.'

'But your mother,' Lara persisted. 'Why didn't you try and see your mother?'

'Because I didn't know where she was!' His eyes glittered down at her with dislike, and Lara was reminded of the night he had savagely raped her, shivering her apprehension. 'After I knew the truth I tried to find my mother, I had investigators looking for her. My only lead was your father, and it appeared that my mother had left his life long ago, that he was married for a

second time. Until the night I came here to dinner I had
no idea my mother was that "wife".' His mouth twisted
contemptuously.

Lara could only guess at the shock he must have
received that night, at the pain he must have suffered
when she told him Marion had brought her up as if she
were her own child. At least now she was beginning to
understand the way his mood could suddenly swing to
cruelty. But she still didn't understand his claim that
Marion had walked out on her own son; she knew her
stepmother well enough to realise that couldn't be true.
Marion had been the most openly loving woman she had
ever known.

'I was stunned that the affair had lasted, that they'd
even gone through the charade of acting like husband
and wife. Because it was a charade,' he taunted.

She moistened her lips. 'Where do I come into all
this?' she asked with quiet dignity, stiffening her spine as
she waited for the reply that would surely emotionally
cripple her.

Jordan's gaze raked over her scathingly. 'You
wouldn't have done, until I realised *you* were the perfect
method of revenge.' He seemed not to hear her choked
cry of pain, staring at the far wall but not really seeing it.
'I knew there was a daughter, of course,' he spoke
almost to himself now. 'I'd even heard of her beauty
because of the relationship she chose to have with her
maid's husband.' Emotionless blue eyes came back to
rest on her. 'I even saw her beauty for myself one
afternoon at her father's golf-club. She was everything I
expected a daughter of Joseph Schofield to be, a spoilt
child who wanted every man she met at her feet. And
they all were,' he added contemptuously. 'Were all after
her elusive beauty.'

'Except you,' she said through stiff lips.

'Even after that first meeting I didn't give you a second thought,' he told her with cruel honesty, not seeming to notice her flinch at this cold dismissal of what had for her been the day she met the man she loved. 'In fact, your interest in me was an irritation I tried to avoid. And I would have continued to avoid you if you hadn't played so nicely into my hands.'

Her breath left her in a shuddering sigh. 'I'm not sure I want to hear any more—'

'You'll hear it all!' he rasped harshly. 'It's time that you did.'

'Your revenge is—over?' She looked at him with wide eyes.

Jordan's mouth twisted. 'It soon will be. There's nothing your father can do to stop me.'

'No,' she realised dully, knowing she had given the weapon into Jordan's hands, that she had unwittingly helped in her father's destruction. And her own. Because she knew that after tonight her marriage would be completely at an end, that this was the reason Jordan was now telling her the truth.

'Once I moved down to London I learnt that your father cared about only two things in his life, his business and you,' he revealed hardly. 'Although not in that order,' he added derisively. 'Your father has always spoilt you, given you everything you ever wanted. And after that first evening it was obvious you wanted me. Badly.'

'Go on,' she invited dully.

'You were everything I despise, a spoilt little rich girl who couldn't believe that all men didn't want her. Your arrogance deserved punishment too,' he told her coldly. 'Although even then I might not have included you in my plans if I hadn't learnt of your twenty-first birthday present from your father.'

'The shares . . .'

'Exactly,' he bit out harshly. 'Marrying you could give me all of it, the means to finally make your father squirm, a way of making up for the fact that *you* became my mother's child.'

Lara flinched at the hatred he had carried around inside him for twenty years, seeing the hurt little boy behind the vengeful man.

'I think that was what shook me so much the night I went to your home with Cathy, the knowledge that my mother had abandoned me to become the mother to Joseph Schofield's child. So I decided that once again Lara Schofield was going to get what she wanted,' his mouth twisted. 'For a time, at least. The night you went out with Gary Ridgeway to spite me was the night you pushed me too far,' he added grimly. 'You needed a lesson of your own.'

'Rape,' she said abruptly.

Jordan shrugged. 'It needn't have been that way.' He gave a bitter laugh. 'Lara Schofield a virgin—I couldn't believe it! Just a little tease, after all!'

She couldn't defend herself against that accusation, knowing that was exactly what she had been then. 'I wasn't the one who told the lies about my morality,' she pointed out tautly. 'I left that to egotistical men like yourself.'

'Only I was the one who *didn't* leave your arms disappointed, wasn't I, Lara?' he derided.

She flushed at the insult. 'You raped me!'

'Maybe the first time,' he nodded unconcernedly. 'But not the next day. Then you couldn't get enough of me, could you?'

Her blush deepened. 'You seduced me into marrying you,' she accused heatedly.

'And why not?' he dismissed mockingly. 'I was just

another new toy to you. Are you tired of playing the game yet?' he taunted hardly.

'Our marriage was never a game to me!' Her eyes flashed darkly.

'It certainly hasn't provided many laughs,' he acknowledged grimly. 'You proved to be so much more gullible than I ever imagined. I thought I would have to play the attentive husband for months before you consented to give me your shares, but you handed them over without one word of prompting. I could hardly believe my luck the night you told me what you were going to do.' He gave a humourless smile.

'I loved you!' she cried. 'I wanted to give you everything!'

His gaze raked over her scathingly. 'I didn't want everything, and especially not a wife. By giving me those shares as a wedding present you saved me the trouble of having to act the loving husband. You can't imagine how glad I was of that,' he added nastily.

Her breathing was ragged as she fought to control the tears that threatened to fall. It had all been a cruel revenge for him, she had never been more to him other than a means to that end. And what of the child they had created through his hate and her love? She would never tell him of its existence now. 'I think I can,' she said softly, her hand unconsciously protective over her slightly rounded waistline. Jordan might not love her, but she intended loving his child very much.

'I doubt it,' he derided harshly. 'It's been hell living with you the last five weeks.'

Lara was very pale. 'It's over now, isn't it?' she realised dully.

'Yes!'

'How far do you intend going in your revenge on my father?'

'All the way, until his business is so tied up in knots he can't move without my say-so!'

She swallowed hard. 'I think you should talk to him first. I'm sure there's a logical explanation of the way Marion acted—'

'There is nothing *logical* about a mother walking out on her child,' Jordan rasped fiercely.

She knew that, knew that even though Jordan hated her, that he had never loved her, that she wanted to keep his child more than anything. 'I still don't believe Marion acted the way you say she did,' she shook her head. 'I can never believe that.'

'I'm not asking that you do! You see, I lived it, Lara, I know *exactly* how it happened.' His eyes glittered dangerously.

Lara met his gaze fearlessly, knowing he couldn't hurt her any more than he already had. 'Would it hurt you to talk to my father, to ask him—'

'I wouldn't give him the satisfaction!'

'Poor Jordan,' she shook her head sadly, her eyes dark with compassion. 'That's just your pride talking. What is it really, are you afraid you *could* have been wrong about the past, that there just might be a reasonable explanation for what happened?'

'Men like your father can no doubt make most things sound reasonable,' he scorned. 'If he couldn't my mother would never have gone to him.'

Lara finally lost the battle to stop the tears as they fell softly against her cheeks. Throughout all that Jordan had told her came the knowledge that he had loved his mother very much, that he had been deeply hurt by what he considered her rejection. She could almost picture the bewilderment of the ten-year-old he had been when his mother had seemingly just walked out on him, could imagine the pain that would grow into anger, an anger that would fester and grow over the years, until he wanted revenge on the man he thought prompted his mother's actions. She could even understand the cold savagery he had felt when he discovered that his mother had brought up and loved that man's child. What she couldn't understand, and wouldn't accept, was his reluctance to talk to her father. Unless he had lived with that hate for so long he didn't know how to live without it!

'What can you lose by just talking to him, Jordan?' she tried to reason with him. 'You've said yourself that there's nothing he can do to stop you now, so what harm will it do to talk to him?'

'I don't have to explain my actions to you, Lara,' he snapped arrogantly. 'I've only told you the truth now because I'm tired of being your husband.' He glanced at his wrist-watch. 'I'm already late for my date with Cathy,' he looked up at her. 'I take it you'll be gone by the time I get back?'

She looked down at her tightly clasped hands, absently noticing how the nails of one hand had dug so deeply into the back of the other that she had almost drawn blood. And she had felt no pain at all. 'Yes,' she confirmed huskily, knowing she couldn't stay.

He nodded, as if it were the answer he had expected. 'Where will you go? Back to your father?'

'Does it matter?'

'No,' he answered callously.

Lara turned and left the bedroom without another word, knowing she had been hurt enough already, that any more pain could break her completely. And no matter what Jordan might think of her, she did not intend to 'run home to Daddy'! She was an adult, was soon to be a mother, and it was up to her to sort out her own problems. She did intend telephoning her father, though; she felt he deserved the chance to explain himself to Jordan that he had so far been denied. She just didn't want to be anywhere in the vicinity when the two men met. She had the welfare of her child to think of, recognising how distressing such a confrontation could be, loving both men as she did.

That was something that hadn't altered the last hour; she still loved Jordan no matter what his reasons for marrying her. It was a bitter fact to have to accept, and she couldn't help wondering how different things might have been between them if he too had come to live with them nineteen years ago. Would he have just been Jordan, her stepbrother, or would she still love him as only a woman can love a man? She had the feeling she would have fallen in love with Jordan no matter what the circumstances; he might even have loved her too.

He looked devastatingly attractive when he came through to the lounge what seemed a long time later—and totally unapproachable, his eyes still cold, his mouth thinned to a harsh slash. His muscular physique was perfectly complemented by the dark evening suit and white shirt, reminding Lara all too forcibly that it was another woman who would know the devastation of his charm tonight.

She stood up with cool confidence, unconsciously proud in the silky black dress, her hair long and shiny, her make-up light. 'This is goodbye, Jordan.' She held out her hand to him formally, seeing how shaken he was by the gesture, his eyes narrowing suspiciously. 'It's all right,' the casually light laugh cost her tremendous effort of will, 'I'm not the sort that has hysterics,' she derided dryly.

He took her hand, dropping it almost immediately. 'You're going to be—all right?'

She gave a cool inclination of her head. 'That's one

thing you didn't learn about me, Jordan—I'm very resilient.' She gave another light laugh. 'You see, I do have some redeeming qualities after all, I don't have hysterics and I'm resilient. Who knows, in another year or so I may not even be the spoilt little rich brat. I certainly won't be rich if you succeed in your revenge,' she added hardly.

Something flickered in his eyes and then died. 'You're still my wife, Lara, I'll make sure you don't suffer any more.'

'Now don't spoil it all, Jordan,' she mocked, amazed at how brilliantly she was acting. Jordan couldn't be blamed for thinking she really didn't give a damn. 'You wanted my father and me to be in your power. Just let things take their natural course and you'll have your wish.'

'Lara—'

'Haven't you kept Cathy waiting long enough?' she mocked. 'I can assure you she isn't a lady who takes kindly to being insulted with unpunctuality!'

'For God's sake, Lara—'

'I'll move all my things out tonight,' she continued in a brittle voice, 'so feel free to bring Cathy back here later if you want to.'

His expression was harsh, his eyes like blue chips of ice. 'Did you ever really love me?' he scorned harshly.

'I'm not sure,' she replied thoughtfully. 'Possibly, at first,' she dismissed coolly. 'But like you I'm tired of it—'

'You bitch!' he burst out explosively, turning on his heel to slam out of the room, and seconds later out of the apartment—and her life, too.

Lara finally allowed her legs to weakly give way beneath her, dropping back into the chair behind her. Well, she might not have anything else, but she had been left with her pride. And a lot of good that was going to do her in the months and years ahead!

She felt safe at the Manor, more relaxed than she had felt for a very long time, with Jordan's behaviour at last explained. She might not like the explanation she had finally got, but she could comfort herself that Jordan's coldness was really nothing personal, that she just happened to be the daughter of Joseph Schofield, that she would have been hurt by him even if she hadn't fallen in love and married him.

Her father had been surprised to know she was at the estate when she called him in town this morning, not understanding her when she advised him to go and talk to Jordan, that the two of them had a lot of things to discuss. In the circumstances his puzzlement was to be expected, especially as she wouldn't elaborate, but it was Jordan's revenge; he had to be the one who told her father the truth. And she knew, without her father telling her, that Jordan was wrong about the past, that there was no way her father and Marion could have behaved so callously to an innocent child. There had to be another explanation; and she just hoped her father could convince Jordan, for the younger man's sake, of its truth.

Accepting that she had never really had a marriage was going to take her a long time, especially when the time came for her to hold Jordan's child in her arms. That Jordan would want no part of the child she felt certain. He might even think it poetic justice.

When her father arrived later that afternoon she felt no surprise, having known he would want to talk to her after seeing Jordan. She only hoped the two men had settled their problems.

Her father looked tired, very tired, and Lara wordlessly poured him a glass of whisky, watching as he swallowed it down in one gulp. 'More?' she prompted softly.

'Thanks.' He held the glass out to her.

Lara chewed on her bottom lip as she poured the whisky. Obviously things hadn't worked out between him and Jordan, otherwise he wouldn't be in this state. 'You've spoken to Jordan?' she asked lightly.

'Yes,' he bit out grimly. 'For what it was worth.'

Her eyes widened. 'He didn't tell you?'

'Oh yes, he told me—'

'Then why—'

'He told me the two of you are getting a divorce,' her father's eyes glittered furiously. 'Now would you mind telling me what's going on between you two?' he demanded impatiently.

CHAPTER NINE

LARA was too stunned to answer immediately, still reeling under the blow of Jordan actually requesting a divorce. All the self-discipline, the calm acceptance of Jordan ending their marriage, fled in that moment. *Divorce!* It had such a cold, final sound to it, like a death knell.

'Lara?' Her father was frowning his concern of her sudden pallor.

She moistened the dry stiffness of her lips. 'Is that all he told you?'

'Isn't that enough?'

She gave a weary sigh. 'But he didn't tell you the reason?' She looked at him with worried eyes.

Her father was impatient again. 'He mumbled something about your not being compatible,' he dismissed disgustedly. 'After only five weeks I don't see how you can know that!'

Lara repressed a shudder. 'We know.'

'Lara . . . ?'

She met his gaze with effort. 'We *know*, Daddy.'

He moved restlessly about the room. 'Every marriage has its teething problems,' he rasped. 'Although perhaps not always as soon as this,' he added dryly. 'Darling, reality has to intrude even on the best marriages, you can't exist in that romantically sexual haze for ever.'

Her mouth twisted. 'Aren't the words romantic and sexual a contradiction in themselves?'

Her father gave her an angry frown. 'You know

exactly what I mean, Lara,' he snapped, 'so don't try to be glib!'

She gave a sigh, and sat down, relieved when her father did the same, no longer towering over her ominously. 'Our marriage is over, Daddy, it should never have begun.'

'You no longer love him, is that it?' He watched her with narrowed eyes.

'That isn't the point—'

'Do you love him, Lara?'

She flushed at the determination in his voice. 'Yes, I love him. But it makes no difference,' she added as he went to speak again. 'You see, Jordan doesn't love me, he never has. And before you ask why he married me I think there's something you should know.' She shook her head. 'It isn't something I should be telling you, in fact I thought Jordan would have enjoyed being the one to do that,' she said with a bitter twist of her mouth. 'It should have made his revenge complete.'

Her father stiffened, sitting forward in his chair. 'Revenge?' he repeated warily. 'Does all this have something to do with the way Jordan has been acting at the shareholders' meetings?' he realised with a frown.

Lara looked at him with emotionless grey eyes. 'It has everything to do with that. Daddy,' she began firmly, 'those feelings you've had lately about Marion, the sense of her presence—well, it hasn't all been in your imagination.' She could see how tense he was, his breathing suddenly shallow. 'Daddy,' she moved across the room to sit on the carpet at his feet, holding both his hands comfortingly, 'Jordan is Marion's son.'

His breath left him in an agonised gasp, all colour leaving his face as his eyes widened on her disbelievingly.

Lara began to talk again, to tell him of Jordan's desire

for revenge because of the way his family had been broken up by a rich man who cared for nothing and no one but himself.

'God,' her father finally breathed raggedly. 'Oh *God*!' the last came out as a pained groan of disbelief.

'It's all right, Daddy,' she soothed, worried at the greyness about his mouth. 'It's all right.'

'But it—it didn't happen that way,' he murmured dazedly, still unable to comprehend all that she had told him.

She looked up at him with trusting grey eyes. 'I know that. I never doubted it.'

His hands squeezed hers until she gasped with pain, releasing her with an apologetic grimace. 'Jordan is Marion's son . . .' he spoke almost to himself. 'After all this time. God, it's difficult to take in,' he shook his head.

'Not for Jordan,' she said bitterly. 'He has no doubt in his mind who was to blame.'

Her father stood up, impatient with the inactivity. 'Marion and I loved each other, we always did.'

'As a ten-year-old Jordan couldn't be expected to understand that. Especially as he was left behind with his father.'

Anger flared briefly in the grey eyes so like her own. 'That isn't the way it happened,' he repeated harshly.

Lara still sat on the floor, her gaze filled with sympathy for the confusion he must be feeling now. 'I'd like to hear what did happen,' she prompted huskily. 'If you would like to tell me.'

His hands were thrust into his trouser pockets, his shirt straining across a still powerful chest and shoulders. Although he seemed to have aged the last few minutes, lines beside his nose and mouth as he relived memories he hadn't thought of for years. 'The first time I saw

Marion I—I mean no disrespect to your mother, Lara,' he told her gently. 'I was very fond of her. But the first time I saw Marion I knew she was the woman I'd been searching for all my life. It was as if I'd suddenly found the other half of myself.'

She had always known that, always realised the perfect marriage her father and Marion had.

'She felt the same way,' he smiled at his thoughts, sobering suddenly. 'I'd been a widower for just over a year the day I went to your Aunt Marjorie's and saw Marion,' he spoke of his only sister. 'I hadn't realised it was the afternoon of one of her damned committee meetings,' he scowled, and Lara had to smile; her aunt was notorious for the many organisations and charities she belonged to, and was still as active in those meetings even now. 'She insisted I stay, told me I could drive one of the ladies home afterwards.' He sighed. 'You didn't argue with your Aunt Marjorie even then.'

Her aunt enjoyed nothing more than organising people into doing what she wanted them to do. Lara had had a terrible job of tactfully keeping her out of the wedding arrangements last month. Heavens, was it only last month? Her humour instantly faded as she realised it was.

'But for once your aunt seemed to have done me a favour,' her father continued speaking in a preoccupied voice. 'Marion Saunders was the most beautiful woman I'd ever seen. I think I fell in love with her the moment she looked up at me with her lovely shy blue eyes. I knew by the end of the drive to her home that I was deeply committed to her. She invited me into the house for a cup of tea, and of course, I accepted. I had the shock of my life when a nine-year-old boy came thundering into the house about ten minutes later.'

'She didn't tell you she was married?' Lara frowned.

He sighed. 'All the signs were there for me to see—her wedding ring, the photographs on the coffee-table, one of the boy who had appeared so suddenly, another obviously taken on her wedding day.'

'Jordan has that one,' Lara recalled abruptly.

Her father gave her a sharp look. 'He showed it to you?'

'Yes.'

'Lara—'

'Please tell me the rest, Daddy,' she said with a shaky smile. 'We can talk about me in a moment. I need to know the truth,' she added forcefully as he still seemed to hesitate.

He gave a nod of agreement. 'Although I'll expect some honesty from you afterwards.'

'Don't worry,' she agreed dully. 'I don't have anything to hide either.'

He gave her another probing look, finally shrugging his agreement. 'The arrival of Marion's son knocked me for six, and I got out of there as fast as I could,' he recalled grimly. 'Marjorie was her usual inquisitive self when I got back, wanted to know what I'd thought of Marion. Of course I didn't tell her the truth, but sometimes she can be very astute,' he derided, being more used to his sister's bulldozing ways than to her understanding. 'She told me a little about Marion, how she became pregnant before her marriage, was pressurised by her family to marry Jack Saunders—we weren't so liberated about unmarried mothers then as we are now,' he added dryly. 'She married him when she was nineteen, became a mother at only twenty. And from that moment on her life was hell, with Jack resentful about the marriage, spending most of his evenings away from home, and sometimes his nights too. I listened to it all with a bored expression, pretended total uninterest,' he recalled grimly. 'I might have found my soulmate, but it was too late, she was married to someone else. But Marjorie called me the next time that particular committee was going to meet, and despite telling myself I wouldn't go there I arrived in time to take Marion home once again.'

'I never realised Aunt Marjorie was a romantic,' Lara mocked, moving to sit in a chair.

Her father smiled. 'She isn't, she just likes to manipulate people. And she had decided, in her infinite wisdom, that Marion had a raw deal in life, that she deserved better. And God knows I wanted to give her more,' he added shakily. 'Especially after I saw her husband for myself.'

'You—met—him?' Lara was incredulous.

'Yes,' he sighed. 'That second afternoon I drove Marion home he arrived back early from work. He was drunk and abusive, ordering Marion about as if she were a servant instead of his wife. I had to leave before I hit him. But the following week Marjorie didn't need to call me, I had every intention of taking Marion home. Over the next six months I made a point of always being there to drive her home. She admitted to me much later that she knew how she felt about me from the first too, that each week she would tell herself to refuse my offer of a lift, and each time she weakened and accepted. She was married, her vows were made to another man, and we both had to respect that. Until the night he came home from one of his drunken binges and lost his temper with her, accusing her of tricking him into a marriage he didn't want, giving him a child he didn't want.' Her father's eyes had hardened to an angry glitter. 'Marion wasn't at the meeting the next day, and when I went to her home to find out why—' he broke off, breathing hard, his hands clenched into tight fists. 'I hope I never have to see a woman in that state again,' he bit out forcefully. 'I pleaded with her then to leave him, told her I loved her, that I would take care of her and her son.'

'I never knew,' Lara said wonderingly. 'Marion always seemed so serene, so happy.'

'She never wanted you to know,' he said softly. 'She loved you, she didn't want you to know of the mess her life had been in before she came to us.'

'She left her husband that day?'

'No,' his mouth tightened. 'He told her he was sorry for what had happened, that he would never do it again. Marion wasn't a woman who had taken her marriage vows lightly, and despite the love she had confessed for me in a weak moment she wouldn't leave her husband, said that her son needed his father. Then it happened again, and this time Marion ran to me as soon Jack left for work; she was covered in bruises. I persuaded her that she had to leave him, that it could happen again and again. She finally agreed, and we both went to pick Jordan up from school, intending to tell him the truth together. Only he wasn't there,' her father recalled dully. 'The headmaster said his father had called for him late that morning, he'd said there was a family crisis and Jordan was needed at home.' Lara's father looked at her with pained eyes. 'Marion never saw Jordan again after sending him off to school that morning as usual.'

Lara swallowed hard. 'Never?'

He shook his head. 'We reported it to the police, and I had private detectives looking for them. All we could find out was that they had left the country that afternoon, that their destination was South America. When the police gave up their investigations I kept the detectives looking for them. For two years—'

'*Two years?*'

'Yes,' he sighed. 'After that they completely disappeared, and we had to admit defeat. Every lead we had seemed to go to a dead end, or else we found that they'd been there only to move on.'

'Jordan told me he moved around a lot as a child.'

'More than a lot,' her father recalled grimly. 'They never stayed in the same place for more than a few weeks at a time.'

'But why would he take Jordan with him, if he didn't really want him?'

He shrugged. 'A perverse way of punishing Marion for the years they'd been trapped into a marriage together? I really don't know what his motives were—perhaps he really did love his son. But Marion loved him too, and not knowing if he was alive or dead almost destroyed her.'

Thinking of the child growing inside her, of having it taken from her so cruelly, Lara could imagine the emotional torture Marion had suffered.

'We loved each other very much,' her father continued slowly. 'But I think you were what kept Marion sane.' His lips curved into the semblance of a smile. 'You adored her from the first, were calling her Mummy within a couple of days. I wanted her to have other children of her own,' he remembered bleakly. 'But she always refused. And she couldn't bear for you to be told about the child she had loved and lost. I think she felt you would love her less because of it.'

'Never!' Lara shook her head vehemently. 'Jordan said—he said the two of you could never have been married, that his father and Marion were never divorced.'

Her father's mouth twisted. 'Not true. No, we never found him,' he sighed as Lara's eyes widened questioningly. 'He had a sister, someone we always knew was aware of his whereabouts, although she always claimed that she didn't. Divorce papers were served to her home, and miraculously they arrived back authorised by a lawyer. Of course, we investigated, but they had once again moved on, and the lawyer claimed to have no idea where.'

'Jordan was fourteen when his father died, he said they were in Hong Kong at the time.'

'After two years, after her husband agreed to the divorce, his elusiveness obviously indicating that he would never let her have Jordan back, I had to persuade Marion to give up the search for them. It was slowly destroying her, and I think Jack Saunders was enjoying her torment.'

'But how could he know—'

'The same way he received the divorce papers!' her father explained grimly. 'Marion wrote to Jack at her sister-in-law's every week, begging him to return Jordan to her. The first letter arrived back here after having been opened, the others all followed unopened with sickening regularity. Letters, Christmas and birthday presents sent to Jordan were all returned the same way. The aunt was obviously acting on Jack's instructions. For years I watched the return of those weekly letters slowly destroying Marion—she even went to see her sister-in-law once, after the divorce papers came back to us. When she got back from that visit, dejected and weary, I had to insist that she stop it, that she accept that Jordan was lost to her for ever. It was hard on her, but I think she finally came to know it was true. The Christmas and birthday presents to him continued, though, I couldn't get her to stop those.'

Jack Saunders' actions towards Marion had been cruel and barbaric, but what he had done to his son with his lies and deceit had totally warped Jordan's life, making revenge his only real emotion.

'Poor Jordan,' choked Lara, her heart aching for him. 'He didn't know about any of them. He thought, he still believes, that Marion left him without a qualm, that she chose your wealth over both him and his father.'

'But his aunt knew, she could have told him—God,' her father suddenly groaned his disbelief, 'I've had the proof of Jordan's identity in my grasp all this time and I never knew it! I—I had him investigated, Lara,' he explained uncomfortably. 'After Rex Maynard I—'

'Yes, yes, I know about that,' she dismissed impatiently.

'You do?' He looked startled.

Her mouth twisted into a taunting smile. 'Yes, I do. Now tell me what you found out about Jordan that should have told you who he is?' she prompted shortly.

He sighed his anger with himself. 'The fact that he was adopted, the name of his adoptive parents. Joan and Arthur Sinclair, should have told me something. It's just—it was twenty years ago, I just didn't make the connection after all this time.'

'She's the same aunt who sent back all the letters and presents?'

'Jack only had the one sister,' her father told her grimly. 'She was a vindictive woman, believed her brother could do no wrong. If she could have seen the way he lashed out at Marion—'

'Families are always like that, Daddy,' she soothed. 'They usually defend each other. But if what you say is true she must have continued to lie to Jordan after his father died. I know she told him that Marion was still alive, but she didn't tell him his mother still wrote to him, sent him presents. God, she gave him the impression you and Marion had finished long ago, that Marion no longer lived with you, and yet she must have known by the return address on those parcels that that wasn't true! How could she keep up the cruelty?' Lara groaned.

'Who knows?' her father said disgustedly. 'Maybe she really did believe her brother's lies, just didn't want to see the truth, and believed Marion should be punished.'

'But to make Jordan suffer too!'

'Yes,' he sighed. 'He obviously wasn't happy with them or he wouldn't have kept running away. He has to be told the truth now—'

'He won't believe you,' Lara said with dull certainty.

'He has to,' her father insisted tautly. 'For his own sake as well as Marion's memory.'

'He won't believe you, Daddy,' she repeated with finality. 'He believes you to be clever enough to find a feasible excuse for what he considers to have been your selfish behaviour.'

'Then he's wrong,' he gave a bleak smile. 'I loved Marion, and without her my life was only half complete, but both of us respected her marriage vows; we would probably have stayed just friends for the rest of our lives if Jack Saunders hadn't begun to show a tendency towards violence. No man has justification for showing uncontrolled violence to a woman.'

Lara thought of Jordan's violence to her that night in his apartment, although she didn't believe that had been uncontrolled. With hindsight she could see it was the only way he could bring himself to make love to her, that he had known exactly what he was doing. His gentleness the next day she knew was due to his seduction of her. Unlike his father, Jordan had complete control over his emotions, both the violent and the gentle.

'Besides,' her father continued, 'he can hardly deny the evidence—'

'What evidence?' Lara looked puzzled. 'Believe me, Jordan isn't going to take your word that it happened the way you've described. He doesn't believe a word either of us says,' she added bitterly.

He drew in a harsh breath. 'This is why he married you?'

'Yes.'

'God!' he muttered shakily.

'He wanted the shares, you see,' she explained flatly. 'He needed them to be able to punish you the way he believes you deserve to be punished.'

'The young fool!' her father rasped. 'I could kill him for what he's done to you!'

'Me?' Her eyes widened. 'It's you he intends hurting with those shares.'

'No.'

'No?' she echoed sharply.

He shook his head. 'Jordan gave me back the shares this morning. It's all legal and final,' he added at her gasp.

'But I—I don't understand,' she said dazedly. 'Jordan said he was going to control you, and that he was going to *enjoy* doing it.'

'Maybe so,' her father nodded. 'But our lawyer says the papers are legal. Perhaps Jordan just realised I could be hurt more by his treatment of you.'

'Oh, Daddy!' She buried her face in her hands.

He sighed heavily. 'And he's right, of course.' He came down on his haunches in front of her, gently taking her hands down from her tear-stained face. 'You still love him, in spite of everything, don't you?'

'Yes,' she choked.

'Marion would have been overjoyed by the fact that the two of you are married,' he said huskily.

'Not for long,' she reminded him. 'Jordan hates me.'

His mouth twisted. 'I don't believe any man can marry a woman, make love to her, unless he feels something for her other than hate. He—Lara?' he questioned sharply at her blushing cheeks. 'You haven't told me everything, have you?'

She shook her head, fighting to control the tears. 'Jordan hasn't touched me since we were married.'

'Not—! No wonder you've looked so pale and unhappy!' he scowled.

'Which isn't to say,' she added tremulously, 'that he didn't touch me before we were married.' Her blush deepened.

'I see.' Her father's mouth was tight.

'No, I don't think you do,' she smiled shakily. 'In seven months you're going to be a grandfather.'

His eyes widened at this last shock on top of everything else. 'Does Jordan know?' he finally managed to ask.

She stiffened. 'He wouldn't be interested in my child.'

'His child too!'

'He wouldn't want it,' she shook her head.

Her father muttered incoherently under his breath for several minutes. 'It's time I talked to Jordan, I think,' he grated.

'He isn't to know about the baby,' Lara warned sharply.

His eyes narrowed on her. 'You think he might want it, after all?'

She looked down at her clenched hands. 'I think he might still want to hurt us enough to take it away from me, yes.'

'I'd never let him do that,' her father vowed. 'He would have to fight us through every court imaginable to get his hands on your child.'

'Thank you, Daddy,' she said tearfully.

'Which isn't to say I don't think he should be given the chance to make matters right between the two of you.

Hear me out, Lara,' he rasped as she would have protested. 'The evidence I mentioned a few minutes ago, I do have it.'

'I told you—'

'Come with me, Lara.' He took her hand and pulled her to her feet, putting her arm through the crook of his as he led her upstairs to what Marion had used as her sewing-room and private sitting-room. He didn't hesitate once inside, going to the huge wardrobe that took up the whole of one wall and bending down in front of the big trunk that occupied the bottom of it.

Lara frowned as he took out the keys to unlock it. 'Daddy—'

'Wait,' he instructed abruptly, lifting the lid.

Lara gasped at the piles of letters and parcels that occupied the trunk, all of them unopened. 'Marion's letters and presents to Jordan!' she realised breathlessly.

'Every single one,' her father straightened. 'She couldn't bring herself to part with a single one of them.'

Lara fell to her knees in front of the trunk, picking up several of the letters. 'The dates . . .' she said dazedly.

'Exactly,' her father nodded with grim satisfaction. 'Not even Jordan can dispute them—or the fact that they were returned from his aunt's address.'

She glanced up, still dazed by the number of letters Marion had written, only to have them returned. 'You're going to show him these?'

'Yes,' he bit out. 'Or rather, you are. It has to be you, Lara,' he insisted hardly. 'If you tell him—*show* him the truth, then you'll also find out how he really feels about you.'

She stood up slowly. 'I already know that. He wanted the means to control you, that's all he needed me for.'

'Then why give me back the shares?' her father reasoned.

'I won't ever tell him about the baby!' she said stubbornly.

'I don't expect you to, not unless you can sort out the problems the two of you have.'

Her mouth curved into a bleak smile. 'I don't think Aunt Marjorie is the only romantic in the family!'

Her father's mouth quirked. 'I can't believe I made a mistake about the emotion I've occasionally seen in Jordan's eyes when he looks at you. It can't hurt you to see him, can it, Lara?' he encouraged softly. 'And Jordan is entitled to know the truth about his parents.'

'You wouldn't rather be the one to tell him?'

'I've had my life, my love, this may be the only chance for you to have yours,' he said quietly.

She was tempted—God, how she was tempted! She would have a legitimate reason for seeing Jordan, would be able to tell him the truth about the mother he had been brought up to despise, to show him that Marion had never forgotten him. The top parcel in the trunk had been dated the year Marion died. Even then, fifteen years later, she was still trying to contact the son she had loved and lost. Jordan had to believe that.

'I'll go to him,' she decided raggedly.

'Brave girl!' Her father hugged her.

But when they arrived at the flat in London it was empty except for Mrs Knight, and the housekeeper had no idea where he was, all she could tell them was that Jordan had left late that afternoon. Lara checked in his bedroom, and most of his clothes had gone from the wardrobe and drawers.

'What do I do now?' Lara grimaced as she and her father sat in the lounge.

'Well, you certainly don't give up,' he told her firmly. 'Could he have gone to Germany again?'

She shook her head confidently. 'He completed that deal last month.'

'Hm.' Her father looked thoughtful. 'How about the house he owns in Yorkshire?'

Lara went suddenly still. Could that be where Jordan had gone? If it was she didn't even have the address. She told her father that.

'Try Directory Enquiries,' he encouraged.

Remembering the conversation she and Jordan had once had about telephone numbers she knew his number wouldn't be listed in the book. 'It won't be there,' she said dully.

'Try the index on his desk,' he suggested.

She felt like an intruder as she looked through Jordan's personal telephone index in his study, her heart contracting painfully at the number of women's telephone numbers listed there. Jordan didn't have a 'little black book', he had a *big* one!

But she finally found what she thought would be the place, at least it was the name of a house—Highgrove— and after checking the book she found it was a Yorkshire area code.

'Call him,' her father said softly from the doorway. 'Just to make sure he's there. There's no point in your having a wasted journey,' he pointed out. 'We only think he could be there.'

The distinct Yorkshire accent of the woman who answered the telephone was slightly off-putting. What if this were just another of the women in Jordan's life, what could she say then?

'Is Mr Sinclair available?' Lara asked stiltedly.

'I'm afraid not,' the woman told her coolly.

Lara felt her heart sink, then another possibility occurred to her; it wasn't Jordan's house at all. He—

'But if you leave your name I could tell him you called

and then perhaps he could ring you back?' the woman offered politely.

Lara felt her pulse rate quicken. It was Jordan's home, and he was there! 'Er—no,' she answered abruptly. 'I—I'll call back later.' She rang off quickly, looking up at her father. 'He's there,' she said breathlessly, badly shaken, her hands feeling hot and damp.

'And?' her father prompted softly.

'I'm frightened, Daddy!' Her hands were shaking so badly now that she couldn't control them, grasping them together until they showed white with tension. 'I'm frightened he'll look at me with hate again.'

'I haven't raised a coward, Lara,' he told her confidently. 'Whatever happens you can take it.'

'Can I?' Her tone was bitter.

'Yes,' he said with certainty. 'You have your child to think of too now.'

'I won't suffer through the same sort of loveless marriage Marion did because of her baby,' she shuddered at the thought of living with a Jordan forced to accept the responsibility of a child he couldn't possibly want, *her* child. 'He hates all the Schofield family, including this baby.'

'I don't think he hates you, Lara,' her father shook his head. 'And I think he'll realise that once you've told him the truth.'

Lara held that hope to her as she made the drive to Yorkshire, swearing softly under her breath as the rain began to fall. Her father had wanted her to wait until the morning to make the journey, but once she made the decision to go she knew it was best to get it over with, that she would only have spent a sleepless night if she had waited.

But as the rain continued to fall, heavier now, the windscreen wipers having difficulty coping with the deluge, she began to have second thoughts about that. If it continued like this for much longer she would have to pull off somewhere for the night, the strain of driving in these conditions was making her back and shoulders ache.

With about an hour still left to drive the rain softened to a gentle drizzle, although the roads were already wet enough to seriously affect the speed she was able to drive, and the journey took twice as long as it should have done. And as she came closer and closer to where she had found Scarfield on the map she became plagued with the thought that Jordan might not be alone, that the woman she had spoken to *was* his mistress. She couldn't bear the humiliation of arriving at his home and finding him with another woman.

The sight of the illuminated telephone box seemed providential, and stopping the car she went to put a call through to Jordan. A cold wind whipped around her in the darkness, the gentle rain wetting her hair before she could get inside the red box. She heard the same woman answer the telephone and quickly pushed her money in.

The woman repeated the number once the pips had ceased. 'Can I help you?' She was as polite as she had been last time.

'I called earlier,' Lara explained. 'Is Mr Sinclair available now?'

'Just a moment.' The woman seemed to put her hand over the mouthpiece, the voices Lara could hear now just a muted murmur. 'Mr Sinclair doesn't wish to be disturbed,' the woman came back on the line several minutes later.

Anger burned deep within Lara, fatigue and tension giving her the confidence to see that Jordan knew exactly what she thought of his desire 'not to be disturbed'. 'Who are you?' she demanded arrogantly of the woman, every bit Lara Schofield in that moment.

'Why, I—I'm Mrs Howarth.' She seemed taken aback at Lara's vehemence. 'Mr Sinclair's housekeeper.'

'And I am his wife.' She heard the other woman gasp. 'Would you please tell Mr Sinclair that I'll be arriving there within the next half an hour.'

'But I—Mr Sinclair . . . ?' the housekeeper sounded astounded.

'And could you also inform him,' Lara continued confidently, 'that whether or not he wishes to be disturbed he *will* see me. Will you tell him that, Mrs Howarth?' Her voice levelled to cool politeness.

'Er—yes. But—'

'Thank you.' Lara rang off, having said all she had to say for the moment. She had eliminated this woman as Jordan's mistress, and if he had any other woman with him her tone to his housekeeper would be enough to tell him that she wouldn't appreciate her being within view when she arrived. Jordan might just decide to keep his mistress there anyway, but somehow she doubted it!

She ran back to the car, her jacket soaked as the rain once again began to fall harder, her hair hanging limply about her face as she checked her reflection in her small make-up mirror. She had no intention of facing Jordan looking like a drowned rat, intending to show him the same cool confidence she had before he had left yesterday for his date with Cathy Thomas.

Her make-up restored to order, her hair brushed back from her face and secured in a tight coil on top of her head, she felt better prepared to face Jordan, if not with total confidence, at least with dignity.

The driving conditions were worse now, so much so that Lara knew she wasn't going to make it within the promised half an hour, putting her foot down on the accelerator with a determined firming of her mouth.

Quite where the huge truck came from she didn't know, but suddenly it was driving straight towards the Porsche, its massive size and weight meaning she would be crushed beneath its ominous wheels!

With a natural sense of survival she veered the car to the left, and the car bumped down the steep embankment, the headlights briefly picking out the black depths of the murky river below. As her head cracked against the side of the door Lara's last thought was that the letters and parcels in the box on the back seat of the car were going to be destroyed by the icy black water, that she would have nothing to show Jordan after all. If she lived . . .

CHAPTER TEN

THE world was swaying backwards and forwards, backwards and forwards, the momentum of the movement making her feel sick. She gave a whimper of distress before nausea overtook her, then her face was gently wiped afterwards, the murmured words of comfort not meaning anything to her as she was laid on the ground.

For some reason her lids refused to raise, and she felt cold, so cold, sighing her gratitude as something warm was placed about her body, wrapped in it like a cocoon.

'What happened?' rasped a harsh voice.

Before Lara could even attempt to answer another man spoke. 'She came straight at me. Then she swerved, drove straight over the side and into the river. By the time I got down there—'

'Yes, yes,' the other man cut in impatiently. 'Have you called an ambulance?'

'Yes—'

'Then where the hell are they?' the other man grated furiously. 'She could be dying—Lara?' Anxiety edged the harsh voice as she made a protesting movement. 'Lara, it's all right,' the voice gentled. 'Help is on its way.'

'No,' a croaky voice answered him—and miraculously she recognised it as her own. 'In the back of car. Letters—'

'They're all here, Lara,' the voice soothed.

'She was like a mad thing,' the second voice mumbled. 'I tried to get her out of the car, but she insisted I get this box out of the back first. It's just a lot of old letters and things. I don't—'

'No, no,' she croaked again. 'Jordan—tell Jordan—'

'I'm here, Lara, I'm here.'

Funny, it sounded as if that harsh voice had said 'I'm here'. But it couldn't have been Jordan, he was at Highgrove, probably angrily waiting for her to arrive. Would he be relieved or just angrier than ever when she didn't . . .

No matter how they tried, a hospital room still looked just what it was, a prison for people who would rather be at home, being left in peace. Like Lara.

When she had finally woken up it had been to find herself in this hospital bed, her first concern for the child she carried. She had been assured of its safety, and drifted back to sleep with a contented smile. Her baby was still alive!

When she woke up again it was to find her father sitting beside the bed. 'I feel sick,' she murmured, and promptly was.

'Well, if you will go swallowing down half a river,' her father teased as he helped her back on to the pillow, bathing her face and hands gently.

'Only half?' she said self-derisively.

He laughed softly. 'So they tell me.' He sobered suddenly. 'Joking apart, how do you really feel?'

'A bit battered,' she admitted. 'But otherwise all right.'

'There are no bones broken, but you're covered in bruises,' he frowned.

Her mouth twisted as she recalled another time she had bruised so easily. 'But I haven't been hallucinating, have I?' she said slowly. 'Jordan was there, wasn't he?'

Her father nodded. 'He carried you up from the river.'

'But—'

A nurse came in and told them she should be resting, and the conversation was never resumed. And now, three days later, she was due to go home, and the subject of Jordan, what he had been doing on the road that night, where he was now, had never been mentioned again by her father, and Lara was too proud to bring it up herself. She had come to her own conclusions about both questions. Jordan had been on the road because he was going back to London, away from her, and he hadn't been to see her because he didn't *want* to see her.

That being in his arms as he carried her up to the road was the reason the world had seemed to be swaying she had no doubt; why he had been so angry she had no idea. Why should he care if the wife he was going to divorce had nearly drowned?

'Ready to go home, Lara?'

She turned to her father with a bright smile. Home. She had only been married to Jordan for a matter of weeks, and yet the houses she had shared with her father for twenty-one years no longer felt like home to her, and Jordan's apartment did. 'Ready,' she agreed softly, handing him the small case that contained the few things she had had in hospital with her.

The bruising to her body was still severe, her forehead still bore the bump she had received when she hit the side of the car, and the long journey to her father's home seemed to shake her about despite the luxurious suspension of the Jaguar.

'All right?' Her father turned to give her a smile as they neared London, grasping her hands reassuringly.

Her smile was wan; the journey had tired her more than she cared to admit. 'Fine,' she nodded.

'Lara,' he said slowly, 'Jordan is waiting at the house. He—'

'Jordan!' she gasped, looking at him with stricken eyes. 'You haven't told him about the baby?' she asked accusingly.

'No,' he shook his head. 'But I have told him all about Marion and myself. He wants to talk to you.'

Her relief was immense that Jordan didn't know about their child, but if he didn't then she couldn't imagine what he wanted to talk to her about. He knew the truth now, what more could he want?

'Lara, he—What I told him,' her father told her softly, 'when I showed him the letters and parcels, it shook him badly. He's changed.'

'How?' she asked sharply.

He sighed. 'It's hard to define. He called me from the hospital as soon as you were taken in, and he was sitting with you when I arrived. But the doctors told us to go home, that it would be several hours yet before you woke up. We went back to Jordan's house, he had the box of letters with him, so I explained it all to him. He was stunned, bewildered, I think.' Her father sighed again. 'Anyway, he told me to stay on at the house until you left hospital, and then he—then he left. I have no idea where he went, or what he did, but when he came back this morning he said he wanted to talk to you. He drove down here early this morning so that he could be here when we arrived.'

'Is he ill?' she frowned.

'No, it's nothing like that.' Her father squeezed her hand comfortingly. 'He's lost his arrogance,' he attempted to explain. 'It's almost as if he's lost all purpose in his life.'

Lara turned away. 'He has,' she said dully. 'Revenge has driven him on since he was ten years old.'

'Yes,' he nodded. 'I suppose you're right. But talk to him, Lara, hear him out.'

She didn't answer, still trying to imagine Jordan without his arrogance. She couldn't. And she couldn't imagine what they had to say to each other either. Jordan knew the truth now, and as he had made no effort to see her it had obviously made no difference to how he felt about her. And why should it? She had been indulging in an unobtainable fantasy when she drove up to Yorkshire, had been hoping that seeing her again, Jordan knowing the truth, would change things between them in some miraculous way. But Jordan had never loved her, had forced whatever emotion he needed to show to persuade her to marry him. Seeing him again could only cause her more pain—and yet this might be the last time she ever would see him. She had to take it!

'You'll come in with me?' she pleaded with her father as she stood nervously outside the lounge, Jordan waiting behind that closed door.

'No,' he shook his head determinedly. 'He specifically asked if he might talk to you alone. I think I owe him that much at least.'

'And what about me?' she asked bitterly.

Her father touched her cheek gently. 'I don't believe he means to hurt you again, Lara. The hate's gone from him now. I'll only be in the sitting-room if you need me,' he added as she still looked nervous. 'But I don't think you will.'

She didn't think so either as she faced Jordan across the room seconds later. Her father was right, he had changed. He looked haggard, his face pale and gaunt, all brightness gone from the beautiful navy blue eyes, the denims loose on him, as was the dark blue shirt he wore. Her heart contracted for the pain and disillusionment he had suffered on learning the truth about the past, and all reserve left her as she ran to put her arms about him in comfort.

'Lara?' He remained unyielding in her embrace, his voice a harsh rasp.

She wouldn't be put off, knowing that although he didn't want or return her love he had been too long without the emotion, that he had to know someone cared about the suffering he had endured the last twenty years. 'You have to forget, Jordan,' there were tears in her eyes as she looked up at him, 'you have to forgive and forget the past.'

'My aunt—'

'You *must* forget!' Her slender hands framed his face, hating the pain in his eyes. 'It's over now. You can't change or rearrange it, you just have to accept it.'

His face was shadowed with puzzlement. 'Why are you being so understanding, Lara?' He sounded bewildered, an emotion she would never have believed him capable of. 'God knows you should hate me! And pity is something I can't take from you,' he bit out grimly.

He still hated her. Her hands fell back to her sides as if she had been burnt, and she turned away.

Jordan pulled her roughly back to face him, blanching as she winced at the pain of her tender body. 'I've hurt you again,' he groaned. 'Why am I always hurting you?'

'I—It's all right,' she said shakily. 'I just bruise easily.'

If anything he paled even more, turning away, his hands up to his face. 'I hate myself for what I've done to you, what I intended doing to your father.' His voice was a muffled choke. 'How you must hate me too! I came here to apologise.' As he lowered his hands to look at her she could see an emotional sheen to his eyes. 'But it isn't enough for what I've done, it never could be.'

Lara was stunned by the evidence of tears in his eyes. Jordan was humbled in a way she had never expected to see—and never wanted to see! 'Jordan—'

'I'll leave you in peace now.' He moved with jerky movements. 'File for a divorce as soon as you want to, I won't oppose it,' he added stiltedly. 'As you told me once before, mental and physical cruelty should suffice.' His mouth twisted bitterly.

'I wouldn't do that to you, Jordan,' she told him quietly.

His expression was savage as he looked across the room at her. 'You didn't do anything, *I* did.' He gave a groan of self-disgust. 'It's like looking back on the actions of a stranger! Only one thing hasn't changed.'

'Yes?'

He drew in a steadying breath, looking down at the carpet at his feet. 'Despite everything I believed, I still fell in love with you.'

Lara stiffened, sure she couldn't have heard him correctly, that this time she was hallucinating. Jordan couldn't have just said he *loved* her!

He looked up, the liquid sheen back in his eyes. 'You're all the glitter on the Christmas trees I never had, the birthday and Christmas presents I never received. If I could change it all, if I could just have you—I'm sorry,' he closed his eyes, breathing raggedly. 'I've made you suffer enough without burdening you with a love you couldn't possibly be interested in. I'll get out of your life today and I'll never bother you again. I just wanted you to know that I'm sorry for what I did.'

The tears he was too controlled, too hurt, to allow to flow cascaded freely down her own cheeks. 'Oh, Jordan . . .' she groaned shakily, 'how could you have done all this if you loved me?'

His hand moved from the door-handle. 'A few times I believed I couldn't, and then—then you would mention something about my mother and all the vengeance would come back.'

Lara sat down, her legs feeling shaky. 'Tell me,' she felt breathless, wanted to tell him she still loved him, but she was still too frightened of being hurt again, of trusting him again.

He moved restlessly about the room. 'Against all logic, against my feelings of betrayal to my father's memory, I found I wanted you from the first. It didn't make sense, and I fought it, but there was nothing I could do to stop my growing feelings for you.'

'You said you hated me, that you've hated being my husband. You—you've been seeing other women,' she reminded him painfully.

Jordan shook his head. 'I didn't want anyone else after I met you. And that angered me. When I got back from Germany and your father told me you'd gone out I thought your seeing me at all had just been another game to you, and I wanted to hurt you, to humiliate you, to punish you for making me love you.' He couldn't meet her gaze. 'Not in the way I did, though. I was shocked to find I was your first lover, too shocked to force you into a confrontation right away. A sleepless night later I knew I couldn't see you again, that I had to apologise and then leave you alone. I followed you down to the Manor with that intention, but all the bitterness came back when you told me that was where my mother had died, when I saw the bedroom she'd shared with your father. I—Lara, what is it?' he rasped as she paled.

'Nothing. I—Could you get me a glass of water?' She looked over to where a jug of iced water had been placed on the drinks tray.

'Of course,' he frowned, pouring her some, watching as she sipped at it. 'Are you all right? Is all this too much for you after the accident?'

'No, I—I'm fine.' She moistened her lips with the tip of her tongue. 'I was only shaken up.'

'You could have drowned!' His frown deepened to a heavy scowl. 'And all because of me!'

'Please go on, Jordan,' she encouraged, sitting back in the chair to lean her head on the heavily cushioned back, very pale, the bruising on her forehead looking purple-black. 'Tell me how you felt.'

He straightened away from her, the bleakness back in his eyes. 'I felt angry all over again. You were right about it being seduction—I set out to capture you with physical love. Only the hate wasn't there for me that time, I just fell more in love with you than ever. That was when I knew that, if I were to carry out my plan of revenge, I couldn't allow myself to make love to you again. Before we were married that was difficult enough not to do, especially as you were so openly loving, but after the wedding it became torture not to make love to you. I became crueller and crueller in my efforts to make you leave, not wanting to reveal the truth yet. But you wouldn't go, and in the end—'

'You used Shala Newman and Cathy Thomas to hurt me.'

'I lied to you about them, Lara,' he groaned. 'I lied to you about not wanting to feel tied down too. I was already deeply tied to you by invisible threads I couldn't break without hurting myself. That night—the night I told you the truth, I knew I had done so much to hurt you that we could never start over again, that even though I loved you any love you might have felt for me I had killed.' His features tightened. 'You were so cool at the end, all I could feel was anger that you weren't being as hurt by our separation as I was, that I had hurt myself more than I had hurt you.'

'Why did you give my father back the Schofield shares? They seemed to be all that you wanted.'

'I'd already done enough, and I—if I'm truthful I'll

admit that knowing how much I loved you took away the need for revenge. Whatever had happened in the past—happened. I finally realised that nothing I do now can change any of it.'

'And the divorce?'

He drew in a ragged breath. 'Any time you want it.'

Lara shook her head. 'Jordan, why do you think I drove up to Yorkshire with the letters your mother wrote to you?'

He shrugged. 'You felt I should be told the truth, the truth as you had known it without any evidence,' he realised with bitterness. 'My only excuse, and it isn't even a good one, is that I saw it all happen through the prejudiced eyes of a child. My parents were my stability, my world, and when it was suddenly shattered . . . !'

'You were lied to, Jordan,' she looked at him with compassionate eyes, 'first by your father, and then by your aunt. How could you be expected to know the truth? And I didn't drive to Yorkshire just to gloat—'

'That never occurred to me for one moment,' he denied heatedly. 'God, when Mrs Howarth told me you were driving to see me through all that rain I nearly died!' he groaned. 'The roads were lethal, and yet you were coming to see me.' He shook his head. 'As soon as I heard that I drove to meet you—'

'You did?' she gasped, now knowing why he had been on the road that night. And he hadn't been driving away from her.

'Of course,' he rasped. 'You could have been hurt, killed. When I saw all the stopped traffic and was told a car had gone into the river I think my heart actually stopped beating until I saw you were still alive. Why on earth did you risk your life for those letters, Lara?'

She met his gaze steadily, unblinkingly, knowing that now was the time to tell him her love for him had never died, not even for a moment. 'Because I thought it was our only chance,' she told him softly. 'I thought that if I could convince you that you'd been wrong about Marion and my father that you might not hate me so much either.'

His hands were clenched into tight fists, a fire beginning to flicker in the deep blue eyes. 'Why was that important to you?' he asked raggedly, very tense.

Lara gave a tremulous smile. 'I don't think I can ever have been as selfish and spoilt as we all thought I was, because no matter how you've tried to hurt me I still love you. I'll always love you, Jordan, no matter what you do to me.'

His throat moved emotionally, and he seemed to be having trouble speaking.

'I've never known you at a loss for words before, Jordan.' She stood up with a serene smile, confident of their love for each other now. 'I don't know if now is a good time to tell you our other news,' she teased as she went into his arms, her head resting on his chest with an ecstatic sigh of contentment.

'Other news?' he croaked, his arms moving about her convulsively, tightening painfuly as he buried his face in her hair with a groan of satisfaction.

'Not so rough, darling,' she eased the pressure of his arms. 'We don't want to squash your son or daughter!' He seemed to become suddenly still, and Lara could feel the acceleration of his heartbeat beneath her cheek. 'What's wrong?' she mocked gently. 'Surely you aren't going to ask me how it happened?' she raised teasing brows.

He swallowed hard. 'We're going to have a child?'

'In about seven months,' she nodded.

'Really?' He still seemed incredulous.

'Really,' she laughed happily. 'Darling, don't look so

shocked!' Her humour faded. 'Unless you really meant it that day you said you weren't sure you wanted children?' She looked up at him uncertainly.

He shook his head. 'That was when I realised the idea of your having my child filled me with pleasure. And I was stunned by the emotion.'

She visibly relaxed. 'And now?'

'Now I'm still stunned,' he gave a shaky smile, 'at the thought of my child growing inside you.'

'That will have passed by the time it's born,' she assured him happily.

'You'll come back to me?' Jordan asked dazedly. 'Be my wife?'

Lara gently smoothed the uncertainty from his face. 'I've never stopped wanting to be that. I love you, Jordan. I always will.'

'I love you too!' He began to kiss her with all the pent-up longing of their sterile marriage, their emotions soon escalating out of control. 'Do you think your father would mind very much if I took you home—our home?' he groaned his desire. 'I think you should go to bed. To rest, of course,' he added with mock seriousness.

'Of course!' She met his laughter.

'Lara . . . !' He touched her delicate features with trembling fingers, 'I promise to always love you, never to hurt you intentionally ever again.'

Lara knew it was a promise he would keep, and she made a silent one of her own, to love this man so much that he never again doubted that he was loved. They had overcome the pain and bitterness of the past, they had the future, a future together, to look forward to.

And when their daughter, Josephine Marion, named after her grandfather and grandmother, was born seven months later, it was into a world filled with happiness and love.

Coming next month in Harlequin Presents!

727 LEADING MAN Claire Harrison
It's thrilling to have her first play performed on Broadway. But the lead actor's interpretation of her work is unnerving. He brings to life her innermost fears...and her secret desires!

728 RESPONSE Penny Jordan
A powerful Greek involves his temporary secretary in a whirlwind courtship—to avenge his sister's honor. Then when he discovers his mistake, he marries her—out of a sense of duty.

729 DESPERATE DESIRE Flora Kidd
When desperate desire takes hold of two strangers, they struggle against it. He, a half-blind man, is disillusioned by life. And she, because of a selfish man, is disillusioned by love.

730 FIDELITY Patricia Lake
Her hopes in ruins, a young woman hardly expects to meet up with the man of her dreams at a Swiss ski resort. Perhaps that's why their sudden marriage turns into such a nightmare.

731 SCANDALOUS Charlotte Lamb
A London photographer tries to sneak some pictures of a reclusive financier. Instead, she gets caught...caught falling for a man too rich and powerful to return the love of such an ordinary woman.

732 THE DARLING JADE Peggy Nicholson
Her careless driving causes a zany writer to break his wrist. But that's no excuse for him to frighten her, blackmail her and make her fall in love with him—all for his own amusement.

733 DARK AWAKENING Sally Wentworth
When a father objects to his daughter's whirlwind romance, the daughter rebels. And within the week, she is living in the Canary Islands home of a stranger—her husband.

734 BRIDE'S LACE Violet Winspear
She has every reason to hate him. But a young woman's plea to a wealthy Greek to keep her brother out of serious trouble will fall on deaf ears unless she agrees to marry him.

RIDE A PAINTED PONY

by BEVERLY SOMMERS
The third
HARLEQUIN AMERICAN ROMANCE
PREMIER EDITION

A prestigious New York City publishing company decides to launch a new historical romance line, led by a woman who must first define what love means.

Available in October or send your name, address and zip or postal code, along with a check or money order for $3.70 (includes 75¢ for postage and handling) payable to Harlequin Reader Service to:

Harlequin Reader Service

In the U.S.	**In Canada**
Box 52040	5170 Yonge Street
Phoenix, AZ	P.O. Box 2800, Postal Station A,
85072-2040	Willowdale, Ontario M2N 5T5

Harlequin Stationery Offer

Personalized Rainbow Memo Pads for you or a friend

Picture your name in bold type at the top of these attractive rainbow memo pads. Each 4¼" x 5½" pad contains 150 rainbow sheets—yellow, pink, gold, blue, buff and white—enough to last you through months of memos. Handy to have at home or office.

Just clip out three proofs of purchase (coupon below) from an August or September release of Harlequin Romance, Harlequin Presents, Harlequin Superromance, Harlequin American Romance, Harlequin Temptation or Harlequin Intrigue and add $4.95 (includes shipping and handling), and we'll send you *two* of these attractive memo pads imprinted with your name.

- -

Harlequin Stationery Offer

(PROOF OF PURCHASE)

NAME_____

(Please Print)

ADDRESS_____

CITY_____ STATE_____ ZIP_____

NAME ON STATIONERY_____

Mail 3 proofs of purchase,   Harlequin Books   2-4
plus check or money order   P.O. Box 52020
for $4.95 payable to: Phoenix, AZ 85072

Offer expires December 31, 1984. (Not available in Canada)   STAT-1